BOOK ONE
SEMPER FIDO

C. ALEXANDER LONDON

SCHOLASTIC INC.

Dedicated to those who serve.

ISBN 978-0-545-47704-8

Copyright © 2012 by C. Alexander London
All rights reserved. Published by Scholastic Inc.
SCHOLASTIC and associated logos are trademarks and/or registered trademarks of Scholastic Inc.

10 9 8 7 6 5 4 3 2 1   12 13 14 15 16

Printed in the U.S.A.   40
First printing, September 2012

Outside of a dog, a book is a man's best friend.
Inside of a dog, it's too dark to read.
— Groucho Marx

PROLOGUE

It was a mile back to the medevac site, and I couldn't carry my best friend anymore.

I stopped and felt the limp weight slung over my shoulder, too heavy to go on. I'd carried him this way a hundred times in training. Two hundred times, maybe. But this wasn't training.

This was real.

My muscles burned and my ears still rang from the explosion. I tried to listen for the distant *wump wump wump* of a helicopter coming in, but all I could hear was the rapid *thump thump thump* of my heartbeat.

Or was it Loki's heartbeat, pulsing desperately next to my ear?

My shirt was covered in blood. Only some of it was mine.

No help could reach us down in this rocky ravine, exposed to sniper fire from all sides. I had to get across the dry riverbed and over that hill.

The riverbed.

Piles of rocks and debris littered the way across. Dozens of plastic bags. Why would there be plastic bags all the way out here, in this rough wilderness, nowhere near civilization? How did they get here? On the way over, I'd run across the riverbed without thinking, giving chase. But now, I hesitated. I looked at the trash and the rubble. I thought.

Every pile of rocks could hide another bomb, every mound of dirt could conceal a land mine. Every plastic bag could be a trip wire. Every step could be my last.

I exhaled. No time to hesitate. Better not to think about it.

"Come on, pal," I grunted. "Oo-rah!"

I was talking to myself, really, stoking myself up. I didn't even know if Loki could hear me, if he was even alive. I pushed that idea out of my head too. My thoughts were a maze, with traps around every turn. Dragons in the shadows. Better not to think about anything at all.

I put one foot in front of the other, stumbling, but moving forward.

The idea of stepping on a bomb pushed the pain and exhaustion out of my mind, replacing one shrieking fear with a dozen others. Loki groaned at my side. Alive.

I had to get him to safety, no matter how much my chest ached and my muscles burned, no matter the risk of stepping on a bomb or how much blood I was losing from the shrapnel wound in my leg.

You never leave a marine behind.

"I won't give up if you don't," I whispered as I walked, talking just as much to calm myself as to comfort Loki. "You can do it! Stay with me!"

I was never much for begging, but just then I looked up at the sky, the hazy gray void over the mountains, and I mouthed one silent "please."

Sweat ran down my cheeks.

I told myself it was sweat.

I knew it wasn't sweat.

All I wanted was to get Loki safely on board the helicopter and get him to a doctor. I knew we'd be in trouble for running off on our own against orders, for putting the entire operation in danger. Maybe they'd even kick me out of the Corps for being so reckless.

It was almost funny.

I had never been reckless before. I guess I had Loki to thank for that. He was the reckless one.

Lesson learned, pal. Look where it got us.

I laughed. And then my knees buckled as I stumbled over the rocky ground. I fell, crashing my elbows into the earth. The elbow pads kept me from shattering my bones. I heard a low groan of pain, just beside my ear.

"Sorry," I whispered. "I'm sorry, pal."

The buzzing in my ears faded, and I could make out some other sounds now: the wind howling through the rocky crags, sweeping the snow off the peaks above me; machine guns rattling in the distance, sounding like a thousand doors slamming shut in anger.

I looked up and saw streaks of orange tracer fire slicing up a far mountain. Alpha Company must be in contact with the enemy. Echo Company was probably pulling back with their wounded. All but the two of us. I needed to reach them. The distance between us was the distance between life and death for Loki. Maybe for me too.

I had to get up off the ground, get moving, get to the landing zone. If I was still out here when the sun went down, the enemy would find me. They knew the rough hills better than I did. They could follow the blood trail easily enough and they could overtake me in the dark. Of course, by then, it wouldn't matter. If I was still out here when the sun went down, my best friend would already be dead. I'd rather stay with him then, meet the same fate.

But other marines would have to risk their lives to find us. *Semper Fidelis*, the Marine Corps motto, means always faithful. The faithful part isn't so hard. It's the *always* that gets you. Always means always. Even after it's too late. They'd come to find us, no matter the risk and no matter if we were alive to thank them.

The sun was sinking deeper, its burning crown dipping below the mountains, the shadows growing nightmarish and long.

I couldn't allow other marines to come out here in the dark to look for our bodies. I couldn't put more guys in danger.

I tried to get up, but my legs weren't listening to me. My ankles wobbled. I slumped back onto the dirt. I couldn't do it. All the doubts came rushing back at me. I couldn't stay put and I couldn't go on. I couldn't hack it.

Marines were never supposed to give up. Marines always took that last mile faster than the miles before. Marines did not accept failure.

But I was failing.

I pictured my mother on the couch in the living room. She was grieving and nodding, sad but not surprised when two officers in their dress blues came to the front door with the bad news about my death alone in some wretched valley in Afghanistan. She'd lost another man.

I hoped, somewhere in that sadness of hers, there'd be a little pride, at least, that I'd been trying to save my friend. That I didn't just walk away and abandon him. Would that comfort her at all?

And then, suddenly, a helicopter dropped from the top of a hill, fifty yards in front of me, and sank to the dirt in a cloud of dust. The dust shrouded everything in a reddish haze, and the helicopter vanished inside it.

I ducked my head to shield my eyes, and I only caught the first quick glimpse of the marines who'd come to the rescue.

Semper Fi, I thought.

They covered the distance between us in seconds. Before anyone could say anything, the dirt all around me kicked up in a tight line of bullet impacts. Two of the guys fired their own weapons back toward the ridge. The dirt stopped kicking up. Whoever had been shooting at us must have ducked for cover.

I felt Loki's weight lifted from my shoulder, felt strong hands pull me from the ground, heard them calling my name, but I didn't answer them.

"Loki!" my voice croaked out, raspy with dust and exhaustion. "Loki needs a medic. He's wounded!"

I felt them dragging me into the dust cloud, toward the helicopter. More gunfire rattled around us.

"Come on, Gus, hang on," someone told me. Was it Doc Vasquez? Why was he helping me and not Loki?

"Forget me!" I yelled. "Help Loki! Get him out of here!"

If Doc Vasquez answered, I couldn't hear over the rotor blades and the high whine of the engines. Someone packed a new bandage onto the wound in my leg, and they hauled me into the bird.

There was a lurch as the chopper lifted off the ground and peeled away from the riverbed, tilting crazily as it sped over the mountains to safety. I felt myself sliding down the metal deck toward the back. Rough hands held me in place because I couldn't steady myself. I was still groaning Loki's name, and I knew my face was streaked with tears. I felt like a child.

The tail gunner was a shadow against the landscape below, totally still as the earth raced by beneath him. He fired off a couple of shots toward the hills to cover our get-away. It felt like hours since I'd collapsed on the ground with Loki. It had probably been less than five minutes.

"Where's Loki?" I called out. "Where is he?"

That's when I heard it: a faint bark, just to my left. I reached over to scratch behind Loki's ears. The dog whimpered.

"Hang in there, good boy," I cooed at him, my voice cracking. I tilted my head back to see my friend. The black Labrador retriever had closed his big brown eyes and rested his snout flat on the deck. His ears sagged back on his head. I felt my eyes getting heavy too. I was so tired.

"Stay with me, good boy," I mumbled at Loki — my partner, my teammate, my best friend in this crazy war. I tried to hold my eyes open as long as I could, tried to keep scratching behind Loki's ears and speaking in my most comforting voice. I knew, I just knew that Loki could understand.

My lips kept moving even after I didn't have the strength to make any noise. I just repeated myself over and over, pleading for one thing, the thing I wanted more than anything in the nineteen years I'd been alive: "Stay with me, Loki," I told him. "Stay with me, Marine."

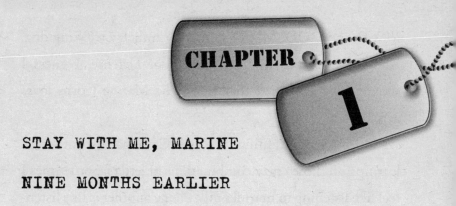

CHAPTER 1

STAY WITH ME, MARINE

NINE MONTHS EARLIER

"**S**tay with me, Marine." Master Sergeant Gipson said it under his breath, trying to keep me focused, but I wasn't listening. I was staring straight into the eyes of the dog at his heel, a massive German shepherd named Ccujo, who was giving me a low, throaty growl.

Before you start correcting me, you should know that I spelled "Ccujo" that way on purpose. All the MWDs born and bred at Lackland Air Force Base have their names spelled with a double first letter so that it's easy to tell where they were born. Dogs born somewhere else and bought by the DOD have normal names with a single first letter. It's just something the military does.

Like the acronyms, all those crazy combinations of letters.

MWD and DOD. MWD stands for military working dog. And DOD stands for Department of Defense. I guess I should have explained that first. The Marine Corps loves acronyms.

During basic training in North Carolina, I spent weeks learning all those crazy combinations of letters. Sometimes I feel like listening to marines talk to one another is like listening to the elves in the fantasy books my little brother Zach is obsessed with. It's like a made-up language. The military has got some crazy way of saying just about everything in a way that only soldiers understand. I wonder if civilians who hear us think we're actually speaking some elf language.

"Stay with me, Marine," Master Sergeant Gipson said again in plain enough English, drawing my focus up to him. I was standing there in front of him, dressed in a full-body protective bite suit, sweating like crazy, puffed up like a marshmallow man.

I could see every muscle in Ccujo's body tensing. The black and brown fur on his back pricked up. His tail pointed back, rigid. His mouth was closed, for now, but I knew that behind those dark doggy lips were two rows of sharp canine teeth that could chomp down with over two hundred psi. That's pounds per square inch, which is a way of measuring pressure. It only takes fifteen psi to crack a human skull and seven psi to break a rib, so, you know, I was nervous.

Anyone staring down a dog like Ccujo would get nervous, even a marine. That was kind of the point. A cute, cuddly military dog wouldn't be much good at scaring off criminals and terrorists, right?

I felt hot sweat trickle down the small of my back. I wasn't just nervous about the dog. I was nervous about the crowd watching from the bleachers.

Just behind Master Sergeant Gipson and Ccujo, three hundred middle school kids squirmed around one another to get a better view. I was really starting to wonder why I'd volunteered to do this.

This was supposed to be my day off, but I had to show the Master Sergeant my commitment. Getting in the bite suit was like extra credit.

So, while other guys with days off were hitting the beach, flirting with girls, and generally relaxing, I was standing in the hot California sun waiting to get chomped on by a dog with a crazy horror-movie name.

I kept thinking of what my mother had told me the night that I came home and said I'd gone to the United States Marine Corps recruiter at the mall and enlisted.

"You signed up for infantry?" she asked.

I nodded. Didn't say a word. I just nodded.

But Mom didn't feel she needed to say anything either, I guess. She snorted once through her nose.

They say a picture's worth a thousand words. I guess one of my mother's snorts is worth a million. It sent my blood boiling. I fed Baxter and TJ some scraps from my plate.

"Don't do that," Mom snapped at me. "It gives them bad habits."

"Infantry's the backbone of the Corps," I said. I didn't want her to change the subject. I felt like explaining myself, justifying what I'd done. "It's where the real men are made."

"Real men?" Mom shook her head.

I had wanted to be a marine since I was nine years old. It was because of that cheesy ad on TV where the knight slays the dragon and then turns into a United States Marine in dress blues with a shining sword. As soon as I saw it, I wanted that uniform and I wanted that sword. I wanted to slay dragons. I had never been much of a talker, and the marines didn't care much for talk. They were men — and women — of action.

"What's infantry?" Zach asked. He was pushing peas around on his plate with the side of his fork to keep busy while Mom and I argued, but now he looked up at me. His tiny twig arms were poking out of a T-shirt with a troll on it, and he had on the big chunky chrome watch I'd given him last Christmas. It was way too big for him, a grown-up watch, but he almost never took it off. It clanged on the side of his plate as he set his fork down.

"It means I'll be a rifleman," I told Zach. "A warrior."

My little brother was just finishing elementary school, top of his fifth grade class, and his nose was always in some thick book about wizards or elves or something. He made me read half of them aloud to him. I'd probably read a thousand pages about make-believe kingdoms and epic battles among monsters and gnomes and stuff. I was amazed a kid could read so much but still not know the word *infantry*. I mean, our country had been at war in the real world since he was born. But he knew more about these made-up countries filled with elves than he knew about our own.

I guess we never talked about real world stuff at home. It wasn't his fault. Whenever there was news on about the wars, Mom would snort in that way of hers and change the channel.

"Like the guy fighting the dragon on that ad?" Zach replied. I guess he did pay some attention when I told him things. Or maybe he just liked the idea of his older brother as a character in one of his fantasy books.

I grinned — I couldn't help it. Gus the dragon slayer.

"What about college?" Mom said, not even listening to Zach's question. That made me mad, like just because Zach was young his question didn't matter.

"Yeah, like the guy fighting the dragon," I told Zach. He grinned too.

"Hello?" Mom said. "College?"

I turned back to her. "I can do college after," I said.

"After they eat you alive." She slammed her fork down on the table. "After they take the best years of your life, chew you up, and, if you're lucky, spit you out."

"They will not." I said. "I'm not like Dad."

Mom's nostrils flared like a thousand of her snorts were backed up in there, hot as dragon's breath. I knew right away I shouldn't have opened my mouth. I should have known better than to bring up Dad.

He'd been gone ten years already, but Mom still couldn't forgive him for leaving. He'd been in the Marine Corps as an infantryman when I was a little kid. He was always away somewhere. I had only the haziest memories of him in his uniform, of him showing up for my peewee football games

14

in his camouflage fatigues, of him and my mother yelling at each other late at night. He'd only been out of the marines for a month when he packed a bag and left us. He didn't come back.

Mom stared down at her plate, her palms spread wide on the table. Zach watched us silently, looking between us for some idea of how he was supposed to feel. I knew he didn't have any memories of our dad, but he knew I had upset Mom and he didn't like that. The heroes in his books never upset their mothers. Except maybe by leaving home for noble quests.

"I mean, I . . ." I wanted to fix this, to explain to her and to Zach how this was a good thing. But I had no idea what to say.

"I'll come back," I finally told her. "I'm strong enough to do this. They won't chew me up and spit me out."

Mom took a deep breath and looked up at me for a long time, studying my face. She didn't say anything else. She just got up and started to wash the dishes, banging them into the sink louder than she needed to.

I took our dogs, Baxter and TJ, for a walk. Whenever people confused me or let me down, I knew they'd be there, forgiving, never judging, just happy to see me.

"Do you guys think I'm doing the right thing?" I asked the dogs.

They panted and bounded around our property, chasing after squirrels and sniffing at the day's collection of new smells.

As long as you come back to us, I imagined them thinking.

I went off to basic training in North Carolina a week after graduation from high school.

Zach told me to kill some dragons and gave me a fist bump. Mom hugged me and cried.

"Don't worry," I told her. "I'll do a good job. You'll see."

She sighed and watched me get on the bus with her arm wrapped tightly around Zach's shoulders. I wanted more than ever to prove to her that I could do this.

But I guess she was right about the Marine Corps chewing me up.

Ccujo was definitely planning on chewing me up.

I don't know about spitting me out, though. I sure hoped so.

"I said, stay with me, Marine!" Master Sergeant Gipson shouted this time, snapping me back to attention. He could see the look of panic on my face. So could all the kids watching from the bleachers. I swallowed hard. I'd gotten through recruit training and School of Infantry training, and I could get through this. I imagined Zach in the audience, watching me and smiling. This was like the trials that every hero in his fantasy books has to go through to prove they are ready for their quest.

"Good to go?" the Master Sergeant asked.

"Oo-rah!" I shouted back, the standard battle cry of the marines. Really, it answers just about any question you want it to. I liked the Corps for that. You didn't need to say much to get your point across.

"Run!" Master Sergeant ordered.

I did as I was told.

I turned in my big bulky bite suit and I ran — more like waddled — as fast as I could with my back to the kids and Master Sergeant Gipson and his snarling dog. I heard the kids cheering and laughing behind me. I guess they were enjoying the sight of me speed-waddling across their soccer field.

Then I heard Master Sergeant Gipson's voice, deep and clear.

"Get him, go!" he snapped.

Three seconds later I felt the furry missile slam into me, wrapping his jaws around my arm and pulling me to the ground backward. I screamed as if in pain, just like I'd been told to do, but the dog didn't let go. It didn't actually hurt, because of the suit, but I could definitely tell I would not want to be on the receiving end of this bite without the suit on.

It was just like when Baxter and TJ were puppies and would play tug-of-war with their favorite rope, slashing their heads from side to side, pulling and snarling and trying to rip it free, except with Ccujo, my arm was the rope . . . and he was trying to rip it off my body.

"Out, out!" Master Sergeant Gipson yelled, running over to pull the dog off me.

Ccujo's tail was wagging and he was panting, a big doggy grin across his face like he was having the best time in the world.

"You did it, Corporal," the Master Sergeant helped me off the ground, laughing. "You survived Ccujo without peeing your pants. Not every marine can say as much."

"Oo-rah," I replied again. He turned me around to face the kids and told me to take a bow. They went wild.

"That's just a little of what Ccujo here can do," the Master Sergeant told the kids. "He's a trained patrol, search, and detector dog. The US Military uses working dogs like him for many important tasks, from guarding our bases to sniffing for drugs and explosives, and even to chase down bad guys, like Corporal Dempsey here."

The kids laughed while Ccujo panted at me and Master Sergeant Gipson took questions.

"Has Ccujo ever been to war?" one boy wanted to know.

"I deployed with Ccujo to support Operation Iraqi Freedom in 2007," he said. "We provided security for forward operating bases in some of the areas of heavy fighting, and we went out with marine infantry units to search for IEDs. Do you know what those are?"

No one answered, and I saw the Staff Sergeant smile. I guess he liked the idea that kids wouldn't know what IEDs were.

"IED stands for improvised explosive device," he said. "They're bombs filled with nails and bits of metal so that when they explode, they hurt as many people as possible. The bad guys bury them under rocks and in trash piles in areas where they think our soldiers will be, and then they detonate them from a safe distance. IEDs have killed and injured more American soldiers than anything else in our current wars. But a dog's nose is better than a human's, and a trained bomb-sniffing dog can smell all different types of explosives, even if they're buried in disgusting heaps of stinking garbage. In fact, Ccujo here loves sniffing around in disgusting heaps of stinking garbage."

He scratched behind his dog's ears, and the kids all wrinkled their noses and said, "Ewww!"

"So Ccujo and I went to Iraq to sniff out these improvised explosive devices before they could hurt anyone. We went there to save lives, and I'm very proud of the work my dog did."

I was impressed by how well the Master Sergeant could explain things to kids. Talking to big groups of people made me nervous. I was happy to stand there sweating and let him answer the questions, but one little girl had a question for me.

"What was it like when Ccujo attacked you?"

I looked at Master Sergeant Gipson as I thought. What could I tell her? It was scary at first, but then, when he pulled me down and held me on the ground and made a chew toy out of my arm . . . well, I could only think of one word to describe that.

"It was awesome," I said. "Totally awesome."

In the truck on the way back to base, Ccujo was in the backseat, sticking his nose out the window while we drove, panting happily.

"Thanks for helping out at the demonstration today," Master Sergeant Gipson said to me.

"No problem, Master Sergeant," I said.

"Beats cleaning kennels, right?"

"Affirmative," I agreed.

I'd spent the last few weeks doing a lot of the grunt work for Master Sergeant Gipson, cleaning the kennels and feeding the dogs and arranging the supply rooms. None of it was part of my job as a rifleman. But more than anything in the world, I wanted to be a dog handler in the United States Marine Corps, and Master Sergeant Gipson, as kennel master, had the power to make that happen for me. That's why I volunteered to do all this work for him. That's why I had volunteered to visit the school and wear the bite suit.

"You don't talk much, Dempsey," he said.

"I talk when I need to, Master Sergeant," I told him.

"Relax, Dempsey." He shook his head. "I'm not your DI."

DI stands for drill instructor, one of those flat-hatted marines who drag us through hell and back at boot camp to make us into the best soldiers in the world.

"You like dogs, Dempsey?" he asked.

"I do. I grew up with two."

"You've been working hard in the kennels," he said. "I figured you must love dogs."

My heart quickened. Did he want me to answer? Was it a question? I didn't want to screw up now.

"There's a new program starting," he said. "We're trying to get dogs on every patrol in Afghanistan and there aren't enough handlers or dogs to cover the need, so they're training regular infantry to be IDD handlers. You interested?"

"Yes, Master Sergeant!" I shouted, just like I would shout in boot camp. It was way more formal and way louder than it needed to be. Even Ccujo in the backseat perked his ears up and looked at me. But I wanted to show the Master Sergeant how serious I was.

Ready for some big time Marine Corps elf speak? IDD stands for IED Detector Dog. And IED is Improvised Explosive Device, so IDD is an acronym with an acronym hidden inside it. It would take one of my brother's fantasy wizards to untangle it all, but the idea is, there are specially trained bomb-sniffing dogs that need human marines to partner with them.

It used to be that the only marines who got to be dog handlers had to train to be military police first, and then they had to write an essay and get picked for dog handler school in Texas, and then, after training, maybe, if they were lucky, they would get to deploy to combat with their dogs. It could take years of work. Now, though, with this new program, us infantry grunts got a chance to become dog handlers in our first year. Master Sergeant Gipson knew that's what I'd wanted all along. He just wanted to see my commitment.

I think I proved it to him with the bite suit.

"I'll put your name in for IDD training," the master sergeant told me. "If you get picked, they'll send you out for the handler course for five weeks. You up for it?"

"Oo-rah," I said, and I rode the rest of the way back to base feeling about as happy as the dog sticking his nose out the window behind me.

CHAPTER 2

GUNNY WUNNY

We started with plastic dogs.

The first week of training wasn't spent with real dogs. It was spent with plastic CPR dogs so that we could learn emergency first aid. There were sixteen marines in my training group, from bases all over the country, who had been sent to this base for five weeks to learn everything there was to know about being an IDD handler. And what that meant at the moment was that all sixteen of us were on our knees giving mouth-to-mouth resuscitation to plastic dogs.

"I hope I never have to do this on a real dog," one guy, Grantham, said. "The breath alone might kill me."

"It can't be worse than your girlfriend's," another guy, Diaz, joked, and everyone cracked up. Well, everyone except me. I wasn't there to joke around. We only had one week to learn everything we'd need to know to save our dogs if something bad happened downrange, where there probably wouldn't be any veterinarians.

Sorry . . . downrange = war zone. More Marine Corps elf language.

See, the insurgents — elf talk for bad guys — they know that they can't win a fair fight with the US Military, so they plant these hidden IEDs all over to try to blow us up from a safe distance. It's a coward's way of waging war, but it's what we're up against.

And the bad guys just *hate* it when we find their bombs before they can use them against us, so what do they do? They do their best to take out our bomb-sniffing dogs and their handlers with snipers. As hard as we were training to stop the bad guys, they were training just as hard to hurt guys like me. That's why we had to learn all this first aid stuff before anything else. Helicopter pilots learn how to take care of their helicopters, and dog handlers learn how to take care of their dogs.

I knew this training might just save a dog's life one day.

"Hey, Dempsey's not laughing," Diaz said, pointing at me. "I guess his girlfriend's got breath just like —"

I gave him a look that cut him off. He didn't finish the joke. He knew I could back that look up with more than words. I wouldn't ever start a fight, but if one started with me, I'd finish it. Kind of like the Corps itself. Diaz wiped the grin off his face.

By the end of day one, I knew how to get a dog breathing again if it stopped, how to pump its heart, and how to insert an emergency IV for fluids. The other guys could joke around all they wanted. I was there to learn.

But the other stuff we were doing was even weirder than giving CPR to a plastic dog.

On the second afternoon, the instructor — a civilian dog trainer — gave us each a metal ammo can filled with concrete.

"These are your dogs for the rest of the week," he told us. "And you are going to talk to them."

"We're going to what?" said Diaz.

"Talk to them," the instructor repeated, nodding at the ammo cans. "The IDDs have been through fifteen weeks of intense training already. Right now, our dogs are smarter than you, stronger than you, and better trained than you. We don't want you confusing the dogs because you can't get the different voices right. Understood?"

26

"Roger that," confirmed Diaz.

The instructor demonstrated the firm "command voice" and the sharp "correction voice" and the high-pitched "praise voice" and then told us to get with our cans and start practicing. I felt like one of those kids at that wizard school my brother Zach loved reading about, saying my magic spells and hoping I got it right so I could transform my ammo can into a dog.

It didn't go well.

I stared down at that can and all I could see was a can. I heard the other guys changing their voices up and down, snapping that can to attention like drill instructors, and squealing high-pitched *good boy*s like they were teenage movie stars talking to their prissy poodles. I just couldn't talk to the can like it was anything other than a can.

"Sing to it!" the instructor told me. "Raise your voice up high!"

"It's an ammo can, sir," I told him.

"Just pretend it's a dog," he said. "Use your imagination."

I guess my brother got all the imagination in our family, because I just couldn't do it.

"Hey, good boy," I snapped at my ammo can, and I swear, if it could have tucked a tail between its legs, it would have. "Good boy" had never sounded so much like an insult before.

I mean, I know how to praise a dog. I talked to Baxter and TJ all the time. I talked to them more than I talked to people, but talking to a can just wasn't working for me. I felt ridiculous.

By now, the rest of the guys were gathering around to watch me squirm.

"Try it like you're talking to a baby," suggested Hulk. His real name was Lance Corporal Elijah Harris, but we gave him the nickname Hulk because he's huge, he has a tattoo of the Incredible Hulk on his back, and you would not want to make him angry. It turned out, though, that he had a lot of baby nieces and nephews and he loved doing baby talk.

"Like this," he said. He slapped his palms on his knees and bent down toward the ammo can. "That's a good boy! That's a good boy!" he warbled.

I mean, if Hulk could do it, why couldn't I?

I turned to the can again, red-faced, my pulse throbbing in my ears. I didn't like everyone watching me embarrass myself. Marines didn't do baby talk. But if I wanted to get a real bomb detector dog, I had to do this.

"Like a baby?" I said.

"Like a baby." Hulk nodded.

I clenched my jaw, exhaled, and tried again.

"Good. Boy."

If it had been a real baby, I'm sure it'd have nightmares about me for the rest of its life. The other guys were fighting back their laughter.

"Dempsey!" Gunnery Sergeant Woodward came stomping over. He was the NCOIC. That means noncommissioned officer in charge, and that made him the boss here, in charge of the civilian trainers and all the classes of active-duty marines training to be handlers. He made sure we stayed shipshape and got through the training ready to join up with infantry units.

He was also one solid, squared-away marine. He'd had the call sign Redwood when he was younger, because he was as solid as a redwood. "Are you telling me you cannot talk baby talk, Corporal Dempsey?" he demanded, right up in my face.

"Yes, Gunnery Sergeant!" I told him.

"What is your problem here, Marine?"

"I just can't pretend this ammo can is a baby," I said.

"That is the saddest thing I have ever heard in my whole life, Corporal Dempsey," he shouted, even though his face

29

was right in front of mine. "That breaks this marine's tender heart! You ever read Harry Potter, Corporal Dempsey?"

"Sir?" I asked.

"Don't call me sir," he snapped at me. "I work for a living!"

"Sorry, Gunny," I said. Gunny's what marines call a Gunnery Sergeant, no matter what their real names or their nicknames are. I would never call him Redwood, unless I wanted him to make me do a thousand push-ups and clean the toilets for the rest of the training course.

"Now, Dempsey, have you read the Harry Potter books?"

"Yes, Gunny. Read them with my little brother."

"You like 'em?"

"I guess so, Gunny," I told him, not sure why we were talking about Harry Potter. This was the Marine Corps, not a book club.

"I love every one of those Harry Potter books," Gunny declared. "I read 'em all to my daughter and read 'em again on my own. I believe that a marine with no imagination is a sorry excuse for a marine, do you agree?"

"Yes, Gunnery Sergeant," I said.

"The woman who wrote those wizard books would be twice the marine you are, Corporal Dempsey. Do you agree?"

The other guys were loving this. I had no choice, though.

"Yes, Gunnery Sergeant," I said.

"Yes, Gunnery Sergeant, what?"

The guys behind Gunny were now shaking with pent-up laughter. I wanted to hit every one of them in the jaw. This was worse than the show I'd had to put on for the kids at the school with Ccujo. At least Master Sergeant Gipson was a nice guy.

Everyone was scared of Gunny. Word was he'd ended up working in the dog program because his superior officers thought dogs might mellow him out. Can you imagine that? Even the Marine Corps thought Gunny was too intense. That made me want to impress him even more.

I told him what I had to tell him.

"Yes, Gunnery Sergeant, the woman who wrote those Harry Potter books would be twice the marine I am because she can use her imagination," I told him.

"That's right," Gunny said. "But we *can* make a marine out of you yet, Dempsey. We will get you squared away." Gunny turned to the rest of the group, who pulled themselves together and wiped the smiles off their faces. But they were obviously struggling to contain their laughter. Even the civilian instructor looked like he was about to crack up.

31

"Listen up!" Gunny said, and the other marines stood at attention. "For the rest of the day, everyone will speak to Corporal Dempsey in baby talk only, understood?"

"Yes, Gunnery Sergeant!" the others shouted. Diaz had a big smile on his face, like he was really enjoying my humiliation.

"And Corporal Dempsey will only respond in a baby-talk voice. Is that understood?"

"Yes, Gunnery Sergeant!" they replied.

"Good to go." He turned back to me. His eyes narrowed and then he spoke in a high-pitched voice that I never would have imagined a man as big and mean as Gunnery Sergeant Woodward could produce: "Gewd to gow, wittle Dempsey Wempsey?"

"Good to go, Gunnery Sergeant," I yelled back, but Gunny just raised his eyebrows at me. "I mean . . . er . . ." I stammered.

This was not my finest moment.

I sighed and let it out. "Gewd to gow, Gunny Wunny," I squeaked.

He froze. The rest of the guys froze. I swallowed hard. We all held our breath.

I was pretty sure no one had ever called the Gunnery Sergeant "Gunny Wunny" before. He had two tours in Iraq under his belt, and one in Afghanistan. During the Battle of Fallujah, he'd earned a bronze star and a purple heart for dragging three marines from a burning truck while returning enemy fire with a pistol in his free hand and a bullet in his hip. He had more ribbons and medals than most of us would see in our lifetimes.

Although he was shorter than me, he stood tiptoe to my face, nose to nose. His nostrils flared just like my mother's when she got mad. I imagined dragon's breath about to spew out, engulfing me in flames.

His fists tightened.

Maybe I'd just crossed the line and was about to get drummed right out of the IDD program . . . or beaten right out of my skin. All my hard work for nothing.

Then he sang out in a piercing baby voice: "Gewd wittle Dempsey Wempsey! Dat's a gewd mawine!" He grabbed my head and pulled me to him and gave me a loud, wet-lipped zerbert right on my cheek, slobbering all over me.

Everyone lost it — the other marines, the instructor, even Gunny himself. They all just cracked up. Gunny was laughing so hard he had to lean against Hulk to keep from falling over.

I stood there in shock, not knowing how to react. I don't think I'd ever been given a zerbert before, and I know I had never been given one by a tough-as-nails NCO in the United States Marine Corps.

Dog handlers were a different breed, I guess.

"Hey Dempsey Wempsey!" Diaz called out. "Can you give Mama Bear an itty-bitty 'oo-rah'?"

"Oo-rah," I grumbled. This wasn't what I'd had in mind when I said I could prove myself as an infantryman.

"I kewdn't hear youuuu!" Diaz said.

"Mama Bear!" Gunny yelled at Diaz. "Let the corporal focus on his imaginary dog!"

Diaz went back to work, stuck now forever with his new nickname: Mama Bear.

The rest of the guys were baby talking to Diaz now too, like his misfired joke took the target off my back. It's a rule of messing with people, I guess. If you mess with someone, you're opening yourself up to get it just as bad as you give it. I kept my mouth shut after that, and everyone seemed happy to focus on Mama Bear.

I gave Gunny a look of gratitude.

"Wittle Dempsey!" he yelled at me.

"Aye-aye, Gunny Wunny!" I responded.

"Grab your itty bitty imaginary puppy wuppy!"

I picked up the ammo bucket filled with concrete. It wasn't so itty bitty. It weighed about eighty pounds.

"Take an itty bitty run wid your itty bitty puppy," he cooed. "Firing range and back. Twenty minutes."

"Oo-rah," I said, which wasn't baby talk, but he didn't seem to mind. I lifted that heavy bucket to my shoulder and started running. The firing range was on the other side of the base, and I'd have to sprint to get there and back in twenty minutes. Sprinting the whole way would be hard even without an eighty-pound ammo bucket in my arms. But with the heavy bucket, this run was going to really suck.

There's an unofficial Marine Corps motto that went through my head as I started running across the base: Embrace the suck.

A DI — remember, that's drill instructor — back in boot camp always used to motivate us on long, hot runs in full, heavy battle gear by saying, "I know it sucks! It is *always* going to suck! You might as well enjoy it! Embrace the suck!"

And I was embracing it now. Running my heart out, my legs and arms burning after only two hundred yards, and knowing I had a whole day of baby talk ahead of me when I got back. But it was all going to be worth it when I got that dog handler certification.

After I checked in again eighteen minutes later, soaked in sweat, my muscles on fire, I set my ammo can down and gave it a loud, high-pitched "Good boy!"

Gunny nodded.

By the end of the day, I had my command, correction, and praise voices down. The instructor checked us all off, one marine at a time.

Watching the guys baby-talk one another and sing praises at cans of concrete, you would never have guessed that we were all trained killers getting ready to go to war.

But that is exactly what we were.

CHAPTER 3

PLASTIC DOGS

We'd been sitting all day in a stuffy classroom, stuck behind school desks, reviewing our first aid and basic dog handler information on slide after slide of a PowerPoint presentation. Hulk kept looking out the window with longing etched all over his giant face, and Diaz was fighting to keep his eyes open.

I had learned in the six months since enlisting that the marines produce three things really well: more marines, confusing acronyms, and PowerPoint presentations.

One by one the instructor tested us on our first aid knowledge. One by one we watched one another go up to the plastic dog to demonstrate that we'd mastered all the emergency techniques. There wasn't much question that we'd all pass. We had worked hard. No one wanted to wash out of the program before we'd even met our dogs.

We were all tired and bored when Gunny came into the room, and we jumped to our feet in a clatter of chairs and desks to stand at attention.

"At ease," he said, and we could relax a little bit. "Tomorrow morning you will be meeting your dogs." He had a stack of files in his hand that he held out. "Tonight, you will study their training reports and histories, and by morning you will know that dog better than you know the backs of your eyelids. Understood?"

"Yes, Gunnery Sergeant!" we said in unison.

Gunny called marines up one at a time and handed each one a file. Diaz got a dog named Joker. Hulk had a dog named Axl. I was last.

"Dempsey!" I came forward. "You're a special case, Corporal Dempsey, as usual." He handed me a file. "Tomorrow morning you and Instructor Maxwell are going to the airport to pick up your dog, Loki."

"He's not on base, Gunnery Sergeant?" I asked.

"Why would you need to go to the airport if he was here on base, Dempsey?" Gunny grunted at me. He shook his head. "Some top-of-the-class marine you are. Standards sure are falling in my beloved Corps."

"Top of the class, Gunny?"

Gunny shook his head. "I don't like to repeat myself, Corporal Dempsey. Your dog is coming in from overseas. It's in the file. Read up and be ready to meet Instructor Maxwell at oh-five-hundred. And wear your civvies. We don't need this turning into some kind of Support Our Troops photo op. I need you back here ready to work by thirteen-hundred. Good to go?"

"Good to go, Gunnery Sergeant."

He exhaled once and turned to leave, stopping in the doorway to look back at us. "Remember," he said. "Your dogs outrank you, so make sure you salute when you meet them."

He chuckled as he vanished into the hallway to go deal with all the other classes of marines rotating through his training company.

We all looked at one another nervously, wondering if Gunny had been serious about saluting. It was true that our dogs would outrank us. That's one of those crazy military elf customs too. The dogs always rank one step higher than their handlers. I'm a corporal, so my dog would automatically be a sergeant. I guess it's so we're forced to treat them with respect, as we'd treat any superior officer. I wondered how that worked, though, since the dogs would be taking their orders from us.

Once we were dismissed from the classroom, I lay down on my rack and flipped through the file I'd been given. A grin spread across my face. Because of how well I'd been doing since that baby voice incident, I was being assigned a veteran IDD dog. (Yeah, I know the elf talk has gotten crazy. IDD is IED detector dog, so why add *dog* after it, right? That's like saying IED-detector-dog dog. But it's just what everyone says.)

My dog was a four-year-old black Labrador retriever named Loki. He was coming in from Afghanistan, flying through Germany. So not only did he outrank me, he'd seen way more of the world than I had. He was the veteran; I was the noob.

I was pretty sure I'd have to salute him.

I stayed up most of the night reading about Loki and why he was being assigned to me.

He had been assigned originally to another handler, a Corporal Eliopulos, who was almost exactly my age. He'd dropped out of high school to enlist, but he'd excelled in basic training and infantry training. He was one of the first grunts picked for the IDD program, and Loki was one of the first dogs trained for it. They deployed downrange together to get one of the worst areas of violence in Afghanistan under control.

They'd only been there for three weeks when Loki and Corporal Eliopulos were searching a section of road ahead of a convoy to make sure it was safe. As Loki ran ahead, sniffing at the road, they came under enemy fire. Eliopulos dove on top of his dog when the shooting started. They didn't have any cover, and he had on body armor. Loki didn't, and Eliopulos knew the bad guys would be aiming for his dog.

Loki survived the attack. His handler didn't.

After Corporal Eliopulos died, Loki was flown to Dog Center Europe, the main military hospital in Germany for treating wounded military working dogs. His minor scrapes were fixed up, and the top military brass decided that the dog still had service to give his country.

He was assigned to me. He'd only been out of combat for two weeks, but he showed no signs of combat stress. The report didn't explain what "signs of combat stress" could mean in a dog.

I hoped I didn't find out.

I drifted off to sleep and had crazy dreams about Corporal Eliopulos calling out to me in a high-pitched praise voice as bullets kicked up the ground all around me.

I couldn't move.

My feet were stuck in a bucket of concrete. A dragon reared its head in front of me and Zach stood watching from behind it, waiting to see if I could slay it, waiting to see what kind of a hero I was. My mom was on a hill in the distance, watching through binoculars.

"Good boy!" Eliopulos called. "Sit! Stay! Come! Dempsey! Dempsey Wempsey!"

All around me, I heard dogs howling.

They were all made of plastic.

CHAPTER 4

DOG DAY

"Dempsey Wempsey!"

I woke up with a start, soaked in sweat. Hulk was towering over me.

"Dude, you gotta go. It's dog day!"

"Unleash the dogs of war!" Diaz played air guitar in his boxer shorts and made screeching heavy metal noises.

I rubbed the sleep from my eyes. The sun wasn't up yet. I was still dressed, lying on my cot with Loki's file resting on my chest. I checked my watch.

0452.

I had eight minutes to meet the civilian instructor so we could drive to the airport to get my dog. I flew out of bed, pulling myself together as fast as I could. I ran past Hulk

43

and almost knocked Diaz over as I rushed to the door of the barracks.

"Hey!" Diaz called out, laughing. "Don't be rude! You've got over five minutes!"

I hadn't hustled like this since boot camp, but I was not going to screw up getting my dog. Everyone else would have theirs just by walking over to the kennels, but my dog was better, so I had to be better. I cursed myself for oversleeping.

"Morning, Corporal Dempsey," the instructor said, leaning on the black SUV and giving me a quick once-over from head to toe, his eyebrows raised. I worried my fly was open.

It wasn't. Why was he looking at me like that? My hair was too short to need combing. My camo fatigues were a little wrinkled, but not so bad that I looked like I'd actually slept in them. What was the problem?

Oh.

My fatigues.

Gunny had said to wear civilian clothes. But I'd slept in my uniform.

"I'm sorry, sir," I said. "I need to go back and change. I'll be fast."

"No time," he said, opening the driver's side door and getting in. "Can't be late. Don't want to leave our new partner waiting at the airport, do we? He'll be nervous enough."

"Yes, sir." I sighed and climbed in, hoping Gunny hadn't seen me leaving in uniform.

"You can call me Jeff, by the way," the instructor told me.

"Gus," I told him. "You can call me Gus."

"Roger that," he said.

We drove in silence for a while. I watched the trees race by along the shimmering country roads. It was one of those January days where it was cold and sunny at the same time. The trees had lost their leaves. Some houses still had Christmas decorations up.

I thought about Mom and Zach taking down the Christmas decorations without me. Baxter and TJ would be on the couch, watching them, offering their snores for support.

"Loki's a special dog, you know," Jeff said, interrupting my thoughts. "I actually trained him myself when he was a puppy, before . . ."

I nodded. I didn't know what I was supposed to say to that. Jeff let the thought hang in the air, realizing his mistake, bringing up "before . . ."

45

The last handler, KIA.

That's the worst bit of military elf I know: KIA. Killed in action.

"I'll never forget my first dog," Jeff changed the subject. "Gunner. He was a German shepherd, big, stubborn brute. I was a Navy master-at-arms, trained at Lackland to be an MWD handler. Served in the Gulf, back in '91 . . . Just guard duty, no combat patrols or anything like that. Different times."

"Uh-huh," I said.

"You couldn't even adopt the dogs back then. After Gunner got too old to work for the Air Force, they sold him to a police department in Texas. I don't know what happened to him after that. Nowadays, they let the handler adopt his dog. Although I don't know about these IDD dogs. The program's so new, it hasn't come up yet. Loki'll be the first dog to go back after . . ." His voice trailed off again. He kept talking himself into trouble.

That was one of the reasons I didn't care for talking. It wasn't that I was unfriendly, like Diaz and the others thought. It's just that I knew once I got to talking, I'd probably get myself in trouble. I could talk to dogs because they didn't care if I said something stupid, but with people, it was just better to keep quiet.

Jeff didn't take the hint, though.

"Of course, I know what you marines think of us Navy guys, right?" he smiled. "Taxi drivers? Someone's got to drive you around the world, deliver your mail, do your laundry. Am I right?" He laughed too loudly.

It was true that the marines sometimes looked down on the other branches of the military, especially the Navy, which was like a nerdy brother, but it just wasn't funny when someone else said it. He glanced my way and then back at the road. Then he turned on the radio and classic rock replaced the need for talking.

We got to the airport in about an hour, parked, and found our way to the special services desk near baggage claim, where Loki was supposed to be waiting for us.

As I stood there, excited and anxious to meet my dog, I noticed the other people standing around the luggage conveyor belts looking over in my direction. A few of them gave me little nods, like we were old friends. One older couple came over to me. The husband had a thick white beard that made me think of Santa Claus, and his wife wore a sweatshirt covered in sparkly sequins in the shape of a palm tree. She smiled warmly and shook my hand.

"Thank you for your service," she said.

"Thank you, ma'am," I told her. Her husband shook my hand too.

"Lava Dogs," he said, nodding gravely. I had no idea what he was talking about.

"Excuse me, sir?" I asked.

"I served with the One-Three Marines in Da Nang," he said. "Our nickname was the Lava Dogs. Long time ago." He nodded again, his eyes looking past me, like he was watching a movie play out in his head, some war memory looping over and over in his brain. They call it the thousand-yard stare. Soldiers get it after they've been in combat.

I felt guilty standing in front of him, having *them* thank *me*. I hadn't done anything yet. I hadn't even left the United States. The farthest I'd been from home was California; the most dangerous thing I'd done was put on a bite suit and get attacked by Ccujo in front of some school kids.

"Anyway, we'll let you be, son," his wife said, steering her husband back over toward their baggage carousel. "Thank you."

"You're welcome, ma'am," I answered, although I really didn't know why I said it.

I looked around and saw more people watching us. A

young mother was whispering to her son and nodding in my direction. They snaked their way over through the terminal.

"Sorry to bother you," the woman said. "My son Jackson wanted to tell you something."

I looked down at Jackson. He was about my little brother's age, wearing a Tar Heels basketball jersey, his hair sticking up in crazy directions, just like Zach's; his arms thin as twigs, just like Zach's.

"Tell him," his mother nudged.

The boy spoke quietly, but he looked me square in the eye, mustering all the confidence his twelve years had given him. "Thank you for your service," the boy said.

I nodded at him and shook his hand. He had a firm grip. He wasn't much like my little brother after all. Zach would never go up to a stranger and look him in the eye and shake his hand. Zach was more like me that way. We kept to ourselves.

"He wants to be a marine," the boy's mother said.

"*Semper Fi*," I told him. He smiled, and his mother led him away.

"That sort of thing did *not* happen when I was enlisted." Jeff stepped up next to me, watching the mother and her boy grab their bags.

"Lucky you," I said without thinking.

Jeff gave me a puzzled look. I felt bad. I didn't mean to confuse him. But I really hoped the dog would show up before anyone else came over to thank me for anything.

"Well now, if y'all want to step right inside here," a perky woman who worked for the airline said, opening the etched glass door to an office for us.

"Thank you, ma'am," Jeff told her.

We stepped inside and she handed Jeff some paperwork. My eyes went right to the big plastic dog crate resting on a rolling luggage cart by the side of the desk. The crate had a wire-mesh door and wire mesh running along the sides. The wires were covered in soft plastic that looked worn in places, like it had been clawed and chewed on by some powerful, persistent jaws. The sides were scraped and scratched a bit. The crate had definitely seen some rough terrain. It had a cheerful red tag from the airline tied around the back handle, and stenciled across the top in faded ink was a warning:

CAUTION: MILITARY WORKING O.G.

The *D* of dog had rubbed off, but the message was clear: This wasn't your pet puppy. This was a well-trained, weapons-grade K-9 warrior who meant business. Just below the stencil, someone had taped down a torn-out piece of lined yellow paper and scrawled on it in pen.

Sgt. Loki, USMC

Semper Fido

My heart quickened. Someone in his unit had written that on there, maybe his first handler, Eliopulos, or maybe one of the marines over there right now, sleeping on the dirt in some isolated outpost, anxiously listening for the sound of a surprise attack coming in, the whistle of a mortar shell, or the crackle of a machine gun opening up, and wishing his unit hadn't had to send their dog back to the states to train some noob.

Every second Loki was back here with me, marines' lives were in danger and the bad guys were able to gain ground. So I was determined to get myself ready to deploy with Loki ASAP. That's as soon as possible. No time to waste.

I squatted down to look inside the crate.

Loki was a furry shadow inside, his head resting on his paws and his haunches curled around. His lips puffed in and out with deep, snoozing breaths.

"They sedated him for the flight when he left Germany," the perky woman explained. "Dogs don't like to fly. Even military dogs."

I watched Loki sleeping for a minute. His eyes flickered underneath his eyelids, and his mouth made tiny warbling noises. His paws twitched, like he was chasing squirrels. Or, maybe, chasing insurgents. When military dogs sleep, do they dream about war?

Loki and I were going to do some good work together, I was sure of it. I couldn't wait to get started.

I smiled at him and rested my fingers on the wire at the front of the cage.

Fast as a shadow, Loki was up, his teeth flashing against his black fur, snarling and charging at my fingers. I yanked them away just before his teeth clamped shut around the wire mesh. He tugged at the front of the cage, slashing his head back and forth, trying to get out.

He let go of the wire only to bark at me, his gums pink, his eyes bulging. The fur on his back stood straight up.

The perky woman yelped and jumped behind her desk.

"Out!" Jeff commanded, and Loki stopped barking, but his lips still curled up to show his teeth. He growled, his eyes fixed on me. *Out* was the command when you wanted the dog to stop doing whatever it was it was doing. The canine version of "knock it off."

"Lokiiii . . ." Jeff squatted down.

Loki sniffed at the air. He must have remembered Jeff's smell. He let out a long whimper, slumped his face back onto the floor of the crate, and fell right back into the sleep from which I'd woken him.

"Don't take it personally," Jeff said. "Flying can be hard on them, especially after what he's been through. Let's get him in the truck and get back to base so you two can get a proper introduction."

I nodded, my face flushed. This was not a good impression to make, either with Loki or with Jeff, who was, after all, still the instructor who had to certify me. If I couldn't get Loki to like me, I'd never graduate the IDD program. I'd be letting down Master Sergeant Gipson, who'd recommended me, the other marines in my class, Gunny, Jeff, and the marines waiting overseas for Loki's return. And I couldn't go back to Mom and Zach like this. I had to fight some dragons first. I had to come home a hero.

I sighed and rolled the luggage cart with Loki's crate out toward the parking lot.

I had no idea how much worse my proper introduction could go.

CHAPTER 5

AWOL

Loki was the name of one of the Norse gods. Vikings and peasants alike once told tales of his deeds. He was a troublesome god, a god of fire and of air, a trickster. Wherever he went and whatever he did, chaos followed.

I looked it up online.

It seemed like a fitting name for my new dog, especially with what happened when we got back to base. Jeff handed me a leash and told me to take Loki over to the kennel, where he had an assigned spot.

I opened the back of the SUV. Jeff was watching me carefully. I held the leash in one hand and unlatched the front of the crate with the other.

"Come here, good boy," I said in my friendliest voice. My hands were open, with the leash resting on my palm. I tried to look as unthreatening as possible. Loki growled a little. "It's okay," I said. "Everything's okay."

He stopped growling and cocked his head to the side, studying me, listening to my voice. His black coat shined and his eyes glimmered with intelligence. I noticed a sprinkling of white hairs at the tip of his snout, twitching as his nose worked the air.

From the kennel building, the rest of the class stepped outside into the fenced training area, all of them curious to see me with my new partner. They all wanted to know what a veteran combat dog would be like. They gripped the chainlink fence and eyed me closely. None of them made a sound. I'm sure they wanted to hoot or something like that, but they respected the dogs enough to keep quiet. Or they were quiet because Gunny was also standing just outside the kennel, watching me unload my dog.

"Come on, Loki," I said.

Loki lowered his head, presenting the collar on his neck. I exhaled with relief. It wouldn't have looked good if my dog attacked me the moment we got back on base.

I reached forward to clip on his leash, and that was the moment he sprang right past me, using my bent knee for leverage and jumping out of the back of the truck. He hit the ground running, all four legs pounding the dirt as he sprinted away.

"Loki!" I shouted. "Heel!"

If he heard me, he didn't show it. He flew away in the opposite direction, his tongue flapping out the side of his mouth like a banner.

The guys couldn't hold back anymore. A chorus of laughter erupted.

"Looks like Dempsey's dog is going AWOL!" somebody yelled.

"That's how his first date ended too!"

AWOL, elf talk for absent without leave. Basically, it means Loki was ditching me.

"Dempsey!" Gunny shouted at me. "Go get your dog and get him squared away. You're running late."

I was running even more late forty-five minutes later, after I had chased Loki around miles and miles of grass and trees and fences. I finally had a chance to catch up when he stopped to rest under the shade of a parked jeep by the entrance. He was panting and staring at me as I approached.

"Come on, Loki, buddy. Come on . . ."

The moment I stepped within reach of him, he pounced

down on his front paws with his behind in the air, tail wagging and looking up at me.

"Okay, pal, we'll play," I whispered. "Just let me get the leash on you and we'll play."

He liked most of my suggestion, I guess, just not the leash part. When I moved closer with it, he jumped in the opposite direction and charged off again, leaving me, sweating and tired, to chase after him.

As I ran, Gunny pulled up beside me in his jeep.

"Dempsey, you are as stubborn as you are stupid, you know that?"

"Yes, Gunnery Sergeant," I sighed.

"You ever think of asking for help?"

"I like to solve my own problems, Gunny," I panted.

"You've got a base full of marines and experienced civilian instructors and you've been chasing that dog around alone for almost an hour." Gunny shook his head. "And it didn't once occur to you to ask for assistance?"

"Don't want to be a burden on the unit," I said. "Suffer in silence. It's the Marine Corps way."

"You listen up." Gunny stopped the jeep and stepped out. He jabbed his finger into my chest, stopping my run.

"You suffer in silence all you want, but you do *not* fail in silence. You understand me?" His face was beet red, truly angry. "You get in over your head here, we all have a good laugh and you run some extra miles. You'll be in good shape when you deploy. But you lose control of your dog down-range, it could get *him* killed and *you* killed and put the marines who are counting on you in danger. Is that clear?"

"Yes, Gunnery Sergeant."

"Is that it? You gonna ask for help now?"

"I guess I have to, Gunnery Sergeant."

He shook his head at me and turned me around, point-ing back toward the kennels where Jeff had Loki on a leash and was leading him to me.

"You will always get help when you need it," Gunny said. "It's time you start to believe that, Marine."

"Yes, Gunnery Sergeant," I said, fighting the urge to look at my feet. I knew I was blushing with shame. I thanked Jeff when he reached us and took the leash from him. Loki stared up at me, panting. It looked like he was laughing.

"Sit," I said in my tight command voice, but he just kept staring up at me, panting and not sitting. "Sit," I said again.

Still nothing.

"Loki, sit."

Nada.

"Sit."

More panting.

"Sit."

Nothing.

"Sit."

Loki lay down at my feet.

"It's gonna take some time," said Jeff. "He seems to have picked up some bad habits. But we'll get both of you trained up and certified in time." Jeff smiled warmly. I wanted to believe him. He took the leash from me, and Loki snapped to attention and followed him back toward the kennels.

Gunny climbed back into his jeep. "We'll give you two some time to get to know each other," he said. "In the kennel, so neither of you can run away."

I swear I saw a hint of a smile creep across Gunnery Sergeant Woodward's face.

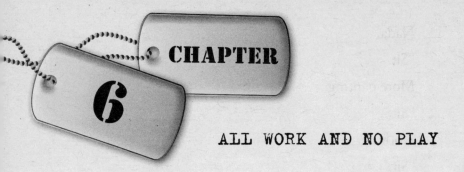

CHAPTER 6

ALL WORK AND NO PLAY

Once we were inside the kennel, I shut the chain-link gate and let Loki off the leash. He immediately rushed to the far corner of the room and sniffed around the walls, sweeping the area for bombs, I guess.

Once he was satisfied that the room was safe, he stood against the far wall, watching me to see what I'd do. I kept myself as relaxed as possible and stepped forward to let him sniff me.

"Good boy," I said, hoping the sound of my voice would calm him. "Good boy . . ."

In a flash, all his training kicked in and he leaped for me, barking and snarling, and his jaws clamped down around my forearm. The force of his jump knocked me backward against the gate and pulled me to the ground. It was just like Ccujo, except this time I wasn't wearing a bite suit.

"Out! Out!" I yelled, but Loki wasn't trained to take orders from me yet. His teeth were digging into my arm, and it hurt.

"You okay in there?" Hulk came running in, hearing the commotion. Once he saw what was going on, he moved to open the gate and help me.

"No!" I said. I needed to earn Loki's respect right now or I'd never get it. I needed to earn the unit's respect too, for that matter, and I couldn't have another failure on my record. Hulk watched helplessly as my dog tried to tear me apart.

With my free arm, I reached across Loki's back and, using all my strength, turned my body to roll him over. I'd seen videos of this move, called the alpha roll, but never imagined myself needing to do it. In the wild, wolves try to pin each other on their backs to show who is the pack leader, and the alpha roll was a copy of that. It was a very controversial technique. Some dog trainers thought it was dangerous for the dog. Some thought it was dangerous for the handler. Many trainers said it could make bad behavior worse. But I was desperate. I needed to show Loki who was in charge.

Loki, however, still thought he was in charge.

He wiggled and writhed, trying to keep me from rolling him, but high school wrestling came in handy and I got him flipped over. The moment he was on his back, he let go of my arm, but he was still squirming. I spread his front paws with my hands and used my legs to lay out his back legs. He looked up at me from the floor and stopped growling. His neck relaxed. His breathing slowed and he calmed down.

"Okay, Loki," I said, calmly. "Okay, boy . . . okay."

"Nicely done, Corporal," someone behind me said. It was Jeff, with the rest of my class behind him. "That is a textbook alpha roll, gentlemen. Firm but gentle. If you absolutely have to do it, that is how it is done." He smiled at me. "I think you can let Loki up now."

I stood up carefully, giving Loki a quick scratch behind the ears to show him there were no hard feelings. He rolled over onto his belly and looked up at me, his ears slightly back, his breathing relaxed. Submissive. Waiting. I knew everyone was watching us and I had to do something.

"Loki, sit," I commanded, and he immediately rose up onto his back legs to sit, still looking directly at me. "Heel."

Loki got up and walked around to my side, sitting again at my heel.

"Good boy!" I squealed at him, just like I had learned on the ammo can. His tail wagged.

"Way to control your dog." Jeff smiled and tossed a bright red rubber toy over the fence. I caught it, and Loki's tail wagged like crazy.

"That's a Kong," said Jeff. "It's the handler's most important tool. When deployed, you will have your weapon and your Kong toy on you at all times. Understood?"

"Aye-aye," I said.

"Now go play some fetch with your dogs," Jeff told us.

"When do we start working?" I asked, eager to use the momentum I'd just gained with Loki to start learning how to find explosives.

"You already have," Jeff said. "You remember when you were a kid, and play was serious business? Well, that's how it is with your dogs. It's all play to them. Playing fetch and finding toys are the same to them as finding guns and bombs. They love it. And you will too. A successful dog team is all about the bond you build with each other. There is no line between work and play. So start playing."

"Oo-rah!" our class responded, and we got down to work. I mean, play.

And for the first time since I had joined the Corps, training didn't suck.

The weeks raced by. The bruise on my wrist healed. I spent hours and hours with Loki, grooming him and feeding him and playing fetch with his favorite red Kong toy. Sometimes I'd hide it and he'd have to search a supply hangar or parking lot for it, guided by his nose and the sounds of my voice. Sometimes I'd throw it as far and as hard as I could, and he'd race from my side, trying to snag it before it even hit the ground. Sometimes we'd just wrestle, and it seemed like he never forgot that first alpha roll. He was always trying to roll me onto my back, to show that *he* was really the boss.

"Not gonna happen," I told him the first time he tried it, his paws slapping at my chest. He tried to roll me with his nose, shoving it into my armpit. It tickled like crazy, and I laughed. Hulk and Diaz were watching us, smirking, and I stopped laughing. I got Loki by the collar and stood.

He gave me one of those looks. *Why'd you stop playing?*

I had to remember that this wasn't Baxter or TJ that I was wrestling with. Loki was a highly developed piece of military equipment. As much as we played, he was my partner, not my pet, and I was a marine, not some goofball kid.

"Sit," I commanded.

He sat and looked up at me with an expression that I could only think of as disappointed. Hulk and Diaz went back to work with their own dogs.

I took the Kong out of my pocket and gave Loki the command to seek one of the training objects I'd hidden. As he ran off to earn his playtime, I glanced back at Diaz, who was rolling on the ground with his dog, Joker, laughing.

Loki liked to work, I told myself. It was all play to him.

Some of the guys brought their dogs back to the barracks to sleep in the cots with them, and even though it was against regulations, Gunny looked the other way.

"How come you make Loki sleep out in the kennels?" Hulk asked me one night.

"It's the rules," I told him.

"Yeah, but even Gunny don't care about that rule."

"I care about it."

"You cold, man, you real cold."

"Gus is the iceman," Diaz said. "Not even Loki, god of fire, can melt his heart."

"How you know about the god of fire?" Hulk wondered.

Diaz shrugged. "*Thor's Hammer 3* for Xbox. I know all the Norse gods."

Hulk just shook his head.

"I'm not cold," I told Hulk. "My dogs at home sleep at the foot of my bed. It's just that we aren't supposed to treat these dogs like pets. They're working dogs. Loki has a job to do, and I don't want to give him bad habits."

Diaz rolled his eyes, just like I did when my mom scolded me for feeding Baxter and TJ at the dinner table. I ignored him.

"Anyway, Loki outranks me," I said. "It'd be like sharing a bed with a superior officer." I looked around the room. "You really want to wake up next to Gunny?"

Some of the guys listening chuckled. Hulk cracked a smile.

"Well look at that," he said. "Corporal Dempsey got jokes." He gave me a fist bump and left me alone.

Everyone else took their cues from Hulk. Among the handlers, he was the alpha dog. So no one gave me any more grief about leaving Loki in the kennels that night.

But the thought nagged at me as I lay alone on my rack, listening to the snoring marines and the snoring dogs beside them. Loki was supposed to go in front to find explosives and to save marines' lives. If I treated him like my pet, I'd be scared to put him out front, to put him in danger. I could never send Baxter or TJ out to find a hidden bomb. I didn't want Loki to sleep next to me because I didn't want to care about him too much. He'd be just another thing to miss when he was gone.

I needed to stay cold. Ice cold. Like a warrior should be.

As training went on, we learned how to control our dogs not just with our voices but with simple hand gestures too. As Gunny explained, sometimes, during a firefight, they wouldn't be able to hear us. Or, if we were sneaking around, we wouldn't be able to call orders out loud to them.

The dogs practiced fetching all kinds of different objects, and we'd reward them with treats or with their Kong toys. Loki couldn't get enough of his. All I had to do was give him a flash of the red rubber toy in my hand and he'd immediately get to attention, ready to seek out whatever I'd set for him.

By the last week of training, we were at the top of the class. All over the base, the instructors hid samples of explosives like we might face overseas, buried in the dirt, concealed inside garbage, or underneath food piles.

Loki never missed.

They fired off air cannons or shot M16 blanks to simulate the noises of battle.

Loki never flinched.

On graduation day, Gunny and Jeff were happy to certify every dog team in our class to head out for the next step of combat training over in California.

Every team except me and Loki.

I didn't understand. Loki might have been a stubborn dog, but he was also one heck of a marine. Was it my fault? Had I not been good enough?

Gunny called us into his office. I stood at attention with Loki sitting by my heels.

"I have orders for you to deploy directly to COP Eliopulos," Gunny told me. COP stands for combat outpost, small bases that the marines set up to send patrols from and to keep areas secure. A lot of the time, guys just called these outposts OP. The combat part was assumed, it being a war and all. The outposts were usually in pretty remote places and didn't have all the nice stuff that the bigger bases would have, like air conditioning or running water.

"Eliopulos, sir?" I asked. I hadn't heard of that base, but of course I knew the name.

"Eastern Afghanistan," he said. "The Four-Four Marines just built it to secure a river valley near the border with Pakistan. They named it after a corporal they lost."

"He was Loki's first handler," I explained.

Gunny nodded.

"They need a dog team ASAP," Gunny said. "Every patrol they send out has been hit with IEDs, and the whole region is short on dogs right now. With Loki's experience and your work ethic, I think you'd be a good fit, but you'd be deploying on your own into an established infantry unit. I get to pick the marine to go. You up for it?"

"Absolutely, Gunny," I told him. "I'm ready to get in the fight."

"Well you'll get your chance. I'm proud of you, Corporal. You and your dog are becoming a hell of a team."

"Thank you, Gunnery Sergeant."

Loki sniffed at the air, and it looked almost like he was lifting his head high. Could a dog feel proud?

"You're from Baltimore, that correct?"

"Just outside the city."

"You need some R&R time to go home, say good-bye to the family?"

"No, thank you, Gunny," I said without even thinking about it.

Gunny raised his eyebrows at me a moment. Then he nodded. "The kennel supervisor will get you all the dog supplies you need."

As I turned to leave, Gunny called back to me. "When you get to the 'Stan, remember what I told you about asking for help, Dempsey. Count on your marines just like they count on you."

"Oo-rah," I told him, and he dismissed me to start packing for Afghanistan.

Loki and I had our orders.

We were going to war.

CHAPTER 7

OLD FRIENDS

"Is this OP Eliopulos?" I shouted over the roar of the Phrog, after we landed with a thump on a dark patch of mountain. The pilot had left the double rotors of the helicopter spinning, and no one could hear what I was asking. The other marines on board turned to me, saw my mouth moving, looked at the dog crate and the duffel bag next to me, and shrugged.

The Phrog is a great helicopter, in use since the early 1960s to take marines almost anywhere in almost any weather. On the metal beam next to my head, someone had scrawled graffiti that read: *Never trust an aircraft under thirty.* The problem was, these old choppers were really loud.

The back ramp opened and guys started pulling out supplies: boxes of ammo, cases of MREs — meals ready to eat — and giant wire frames called HESCOs that would be filled with dirt and used to create bulletproof, bombproof walls. I groaned at the thought that I, as the new guy, might be the one with the shovel filling them.

Of course, I still didn't know if I was in the right place. I'd been traveling for almost a week to get to the outpost. I had to fly on a normal airplane to Europe, and then take a military jet to the big base at Camp Leatherneck, and then I had to wait around for two days, trying to keep Loki busy, until the weather cleared in the mountains and a helicopter made a supply run to a few of the outposts near the border. It wasn't like riding the bus. There were no signs telling me if this was my stop.

"Eliopulos?" I yelled at the crew chief, who was trying to get the marines from the base to unload all the cargo faster so the Phrog could take off again. They landed at night because it was harder for enemy snipers to shoot down the helicopters.

Harder, but not impossible.

The crew chief sort of nodded. It seemed like a yes, so I grabbed my duffel and threw it to the dirt.

The other marines didn't even look my way. They just carried their supplies across the small LZ — that's military elf for landing zone — and down some rough steps carved into the dirt. They vanished into a bunker and didn't reappear.

I hauled Loki's big crate off the helicopter, and the crew chief stuck his finger in the air and made a twirling motion. He stepped up on the ramp, which wasn't even closed as they took off again, veering hard sideways toward the next outpost farther down the valley.

I was left on the landing pad, listening to the whapping sound of the helicopter's blades fade away. The mountain air was so cold, I could see my breath. I heard Loki whine in his crate.

I took off my helmet and bent down to offer him some comforting words. He was shivering inside the crate. A shiver ran through my body too, but not because of the cold. I really hoped this was the right place.

We were alone on top of a mountain in a far corner of Afghanistan and I had no idea where we were or if anyone was waiting for us. It felt eerie, like I'd wandered into school on a Sunday. Everything looked just like a military outpost should, but there were no people around to make the place feel right.

"You the IDD team?" someone called out to me, a head popping up over the edge of the landing zone from the dirt steps into the trench below. He was wearing a knit watch cap but no shirt. He had a broad chest with a nasty scar wrapped all the way around it, like someone had taken a giant can opener to him.

"Corporal Gus Dempsey," I said, not sure if I should salute or not. I didn't even know if I was talking to an officer.

"Well you better get down here before some goat herder decides to take a shot at you," the guy told me.

I looked to the mountains and thought about snipers watching me through their rifle sights. I knew dog teams were a target for the bad guys. I quickly put my helmet back on, grabbed my duffel, and dragged Loki in his crate toward the stairs. I didn't want to let him out where "some goat herder" could take a shot at him. I hadn't even realized we were at war with goat herders.

When I reached the steps, the guy stepped back, letting me haul my gear and the crate into the narrow fortified trench at the bottom of the steps. He led me straight into a small bunker, where he had a radio set up on a little wooden table with an M16 leaning against it. An opening on the other side led to the rest of the outpost.

"This OP Eliopulos?" I confirmed, hoping I was in the

right place. I didn't want to be stuck here waiting for a helicopter to come back.

"Is that where we are?" the guy said. "No wonder room service has been so bad. I haven't gotten a chocolate on my pillow yet!"

Everyone's a comedian, I thought.

"Corporal Gus Dempsey and Military Working Dog Loki reporting for duty," I said, trying to sound official so maybe he'd tell me where I was supposed to go and what I was supposed to do.

"Oh mercy!" He suddenly smiled wide, his teeth lighting up bright white against the darkness. "O.G. Loki in da house!"

He bent down and put his fingers right through the mesh of the crate. "Why didn't you say you had the O.G. wit' you?"

"Careful," I warned. "Loki doesn't like it when strangers —" Loki was already licking the marine's fingers and going crazy, whining to be let out. I could see his eyes shining up at me like black marbles, pleading to play.

"Oh, O.G. and I go way back," the marine said. "Original Gangsta!" he laughed. "Who you think scratched out the *D* on your crate?"

"You?" I tried.

"Douglass," he said. "Private Lincoln Douglass."

"Like Abraham Lincoln and — ?"

"Yeah, Frederick Douglass," he said. "My mom's a history teacher. It just worked out that way. Now let me see my boy here."

I opened up the crate and Loki jumped right on top of Private Douglass, pushing him back against the wall of sandbags and smothering him with licks. He'd never kissed me like that. I guess I had never let him.

"Okay, Loki. Out," I said.

Loki looked back at me like I'd just ordered him to fly a helicopter. It was a look that said, *I understand you, but it ain't gonna happen.* He turned back and started licking Private Douglass again.

"Loki!" I snapped. "Out!"

Loki slowly climbed off Douglass and sat down next to me, his ears pinned back, his tail tucked, his expression pitiful. Douglass looked up at me with about the same expression. He sighed and pushed himself to his feet. I couldn't believe he wasn't shivering without a shirt on. It had to be below freezing out here.

"Guess we better go see Lieutenant Schu," he said. He gave me a look up and down, taking in my uniform, my stance, my gear — everything regulation, every bit squared away. I could tell what he was thinking. I'd seen the look before. "That's Lieutenant Schumacher," he clarified, leading me through the bunker to the rest of the base.

As my eyes adjusted to the dark, I began to take in my new home for the next six months. Outpost Eliopulos was a collection of bunkers, tents, sandbags, and razor wire stretched up the side of a medium-sized mountain on the edge of a river valley. The helicopter pad with the trench around it sat at the lowest point of the base, which rose from there, up the steep slopes — so steep in places that the marines had tied guide ropes to hold on to.

Nearest to the LZ was the medical tent. A mess tent for preparing hot meals once a week was just up from there, and then there were a few brick barracks dug into the dirt. Beyond them was a maze of sandbags, leading to bunkers with good views of the valley below. Machine gun and mortar positions, mostly. Camouflage netting was strung every which way, to make the exact layout of the base harder to see from a distance.

Inside the bunkers, I could make out the shapes of the marines on watch, lying at their guns, staring into the dark.

"That the dog team?" someone whispered.

"Forget the dog," someone else responded. "Did they bring my Twinkies in on that bird?"

"I look like your mailman, Chang?" Douglass responded. "And yeah, it's the dog team. O.G. himself!"

"Loki!" the guy named Chang whisper-shouted and scurried down the slope toward us. Loki's tail started wagging and he licked his lips, dancing from paw to paw, like he was about to give Chang the same treatment he'd given Douglass. I tightened his leash.

"Sit," I commanded. He whimpered and sat, then popped up again the moment his butt touched the earth. He dove for Chang, but I held him back. He wasn't the unit pet.

Chang stopped short and looked at me for the first time. I saw his eyes dart over to Douglass before he made eye contact with me.

"I don't want to overexcite Loki," I explained to him, but he could tell that I was just being strict.

"Well, at least someone's excited," Chang said. "I'm bored out of my mind tonight. Nothing's happened for days. I really miss the sound of a machine gun fired in anger."

"Hey, Chang!" the other voice from the bunker called down to us. "Get back up here. You can say hi to your girlfriend later."

Chang shook his head. "Later, dog team," he said and scrambled back up the slope to his gun position.

"Come on," Douglass said, leading me farther up the slope. We approached a plywood building with netting strung over the door. A dim light peeked out from behind the plywood door, which was probably why the netting was hung. Wouldn't want enemy mortar teams locking in on a night-light and blowing the whole building away.

"Looks like Lieutenant Schu's awake." Douglass pointed. "Welcome to OPE."

He turned and strolled back down the hill toward the LZ bunker, like he didn't have a care in the world.

Loki looked up at me, questioning. I couldn't tell if he wondered why we were still out in the cold, or why I wasn't letting him play with his old friends.

In training, I'd learned to read his body language during a search, but standing on a freezing mountaintop outside company headquarters, I couldn't tell what he was thinking.

"Here we go, boy," I told him. "Make me proud."

As we approached the door, my boot brushed against

some bottle caps hanging on a string, which made a tinkling sound. The door opened to reveal Lieutenant Schumacher, a skinny marine with a shiny silver bar on his collar. He had close-cropped blond hair and dark circles under his eyes. Behind him, against the far wall of the room, a beefy staff sergeant leaned over a table, studying a map. Lieutenant Schumacher stared at me a moment in the dark, his face grim, revealing nothing, waiting for me to get down to business. I liked him immediately.

"Corporal Dempsey and Military Working Dog Loki reporting as ordered, sir." I saluted him.

He cracked a smile.

"Loki's back?" He looked down at my dog but didn't move to pet him. He just nodded and invited us in the headquarters building. "Staff Sergeant Luken," he said, introducing me to the big guy standing over the map. "We sure are glad to see you two. We've been hurting out here for a dog team. Every patrol we send out gets hit with IEDs, and we've got reports of all the other companies in the region saying the same thing. If you're up for it, we'll get you out on patrol first thing in the morning."

"Yes, sir," I said. "Can't wait."

"We're a small company, you'll find, but fierce. Everyone pulls his weight on this hill, myself included. We all get patrols. We all get watch duty, and we all clean the latrines. I'll keep your rotation as light as I can, so you'll have time to train with your dog, but we've got enemy fighters all over this valley and more slipping in over the border every day, so there's a lot of work to do."

"Oo-rah," I said.

"That's what I like to hear," the lieutenant nodded. "Staff Sergeant Luken will get you squared away in the barracks, and we'll see you here at oh-five-hundred."

Great, I thought. *I'll get three hours of sleep if I'm lucky.*

"And Loki?" I asked.

Lieutenant Schumacher stared at me. "What about him?" he finally asked.

"Where will he sleep?" I asked. "Where's the kennel?"

Staff Sergeant Luken laughed behind the lieutenant.

"Hate to break it to you, Corporal, but you aren't at Camp Leatherneck and you aren't at Club Med. We've got no kennel here. You bunk with your dog."

"Sir, respectfully, IDD dogs and handlers are not supposed to bunk together." I considered whether I should explain to him the dangers of treating a military working dog like a pet.

"Our previous handler had no problem with it," Lieutenant Schumacher said.

"Yes, but I've noticed that Loki has many bad habits acquired from the previous handler . . ." I stopped myself.

Staff Sergeant Luken was staring me down.

Lieutenant Schumacher looked like he'd just eaten a raw onion.

Eliopulos had trained with this company, served with this company, and died fighting with them. He was Lieutenant Schumacher's marine, and here I was, the new guy, insulting his memory, saying he'd given his dog bad habits. That's why I hated trying to explain myself. I was no good at talking.

Any good feelings the lieutenant had for me were gone. First impressions were hard to undo. So far, I'd been at the outpost for less than an hour, and I'd earned the dislike of at least two grunts, the staff sergeant, and my commanding officer.

Only one hundred and eighty days to go.

"You bunk with your dog," Lieutenant Schumacher repeated, and he nodded at the staff sergeant to show me my bunker. "See you at oh-five-hundred."

"Yes, sir," I said, and followed the staff sergeant with Loki at my heel. He didn't move with his usual bounce. His head hung low and his ears sagged. I guess my embarrassment traveled down-leash to him.

I hoped we could redeem ourselves in the morning on our first combat patrol.

CHAPTER 8

DARK NIGHT

The staff sergeant didn't talk as he led Loki and me to the narrow brick building wedged into the mountainside that we were supposed to call home for the next six months.

"I'll have the dog food and supplies that flew in with you stowed in the mess hall," he said just before we stepped inside. "There's no room in here."

The building was dark and overheated by a stove at the far end. Rows of narrow wooden racks — Marine Corps elf talk for beds — lined the walls with an aisle between, so narrow that you could reach your arm out and touch the guy sleeping across from you. There were boots and sneakers all over the floor, and some of the racks had photos and pictures torn from magazines stuck to the walls around them. A few empty cans of energy drink littered the floor. It looked almost like my little brother's room at home.

If it weren't for the weapons.

Rifles and machine guns were propped against the beds or shoved into corners. Every spare inch of floor was covered in ammunition cans. Belts of ammunition hung from nails on the walls and on the bed frames. Grenades hung from the ceiling beams.

About half of the racks were full, lumps under blankets rising and falling with every breath. A few of the guys were actually sleeping curled up with their guns.

The place looked like the messy playroom of maniac children, but it smelled like the gym locker room at the end of the school year, a mixture of old socks and sweat and a whole stew of mysterious men-at-war stenches.

Staff Sergeant Luken pointed at an empty rack right next to the door, the coldest spot in the barracks. I worried that guys would be walking in and out past me all night as they traded shifts or went to the bathroom. There wasn't much room, and I didn't want anyone to step on Loki.

But I didn't say anything. Talking had gotten me in enough trouble. I'd make do with the situation as it was. That was the Marine Corps way.

The staff sergeant saw me toss my stuff down, grunted once, and left. I heard some guys snoring. A few shifted in their racks.

Loki cocked his head to the side and listened. His nostrils twitched, taking in all the smells and sounds. Someone farted, and Loki's ears perked up. For a dog, the barracks must have smelled amazing. For a human, they were barely tolerable.

I took off my body armor and helmet and sat down on the edge of my rack.

"Welcome home," I whispered to Loki and scratched behind his ears. He immediately jumped up onto the bed, spun in a circle, and lay down in the middle of it. He stretched all four paws and almost pushed me off.

"No way, pal," I said, scooping him in my arms, hefting all seventy pounds of him up and setting him on the floor. "Humans get the beds."

He looked up at me, his eyebrows cocked sideways in what I knew was his cutest begging look.

"Don't pull rank on me," I told him. "The cute act is unbecoming of a sergeant in the United States Marine Corps."

He hung his head.

He'd had a hard day of travel, and he'd been a pretty good boy the whole time. I couldn't totally resist that look of his. Tired as I was, I figured I could take the time for a little bit of fun.

I rummaged in my bag and found a brush, bent down, and ran it through his fur. Grooming, Jeff had told us, helps form a bond between a handler and his dog. And the dogs loved it.

So I groomed. I checked his paws to make sure the paw pads and claws were in good shape. I rubbed his belly and gave him a rawhide bone I'd been carrying, which he happily gnawed at on the floor while I brushed him.

I told myself I was doing it for him, but really, grooming him relaxed me. I wasn't going to be able to sleep anyway, and while I was taking care of Loki, I could almost forget that I was the odd man out in an experienced infantry company on top of a mountain in Afghanistan. I could almost forget that my dog had more friends here than I did. I could almost forget that I'd be going on my first combat mission in the morning.

"So, I heard you're going on your first combat mission in the morning," Chang whispered as he came into the barracks and sat on the edge of my bed. "First platoon. We're the best there is."

"Uh-huh," I said, watching Chang as he started rubbing Loki's belly without even asking my permission. Loki's tongue lolled out of his mouth, hanging all the way to the floor. He rolled over onto his back, loving the attention.

"New guy's always on point, you know," Chang told me, meaning I'd be the one walking at the front of the platoon, the most dangerous position.

"Uh-huh," I said again. I had figured I'd be on point before Chang told me, since I was the one with the bomb-sniffing dog. I didn't need him telling me my job.

"Name's Chang," he told me. "They call me Lucky Chang 'cause I stepped on a land mine once and it didn't go off."

I nodded.

"You don't say much," he said.

I nodded again.

"I heard you talking to the dog," he said. "More a dog person than a people person, eh?"

"I guess so," I told him.

"That's cool. I got a dog at home, back in Brooklyn. Little Chihuahua. It was my girlfriend's. She dumped me for

88

some club promoter but left the dog. My mom's looking after it. I miss that girl." He sighed. "I mean the dog, not the girlfriend."

He waited for me to laugh. I gave him a smile, which was the best I could do at the moment. I wasn't in a joking mood.

"Why so serious . . . ?" Chang croaked at me. He raised his eyebrows when I didn't respond. "The Joker? From *The Dark Knight*? It's not my best impression, but come on. Throw me a bone here. You can't be that gung ho, can you?"

"I'm whatever Gotham needs me to be," I said, doing my own Batman impression.

Chang didn't respond. I guess impressions weren't my thing. He slipped off my rack, kneeling to give Loki one last pat on the belly. "Tell your master to lighten up," he told Loki. "Life's too short . . . especially up here." He looked up at me. "See you in the morning, Batman." He chuckled and wandered back to his own rack.

I lay on my back and stared up at the low metal ceiling of the barracks building, thinking about how I'd do on my first combat patrol, thinking about how Loki would do. He was a goofball, but he was good enough at his job that they'd sent him back here with me, noob that I was. I just hoped I could control him and hoped that I wouldn't let my new platoon down. Mistakes could be deadly out here. I had to prove that I could handle it, that I could be useful and that I deserved to be here. They'd named the outpost after the guy I was replacing. He'd made the ultimate sacrifice. How could I ever live up to that?

I heard Loki snoring on the floor, about as loud as some of the other marines.

I wondered if Loki understood what had happened to Eliopulos. I wondered if TJ and Baxter knew where I'd gone. I wondered if dogs could grieve.

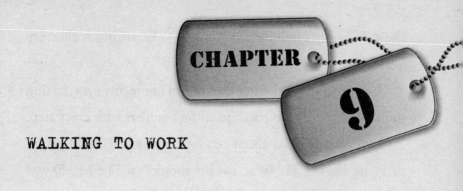

CHAPTER 9

WALKING TO WORK

It was still dark when we set out on foot from the outpost.

I was in front, with Loki walking by my side on a leash attached to my belt. My M16 hung by its strap in front of my chest. I had on my body armor, my Kevlar helmet, a full CamelBak of water on my back, extra ammo magazines on my chest, and Loki's toy tucked away in a front pocket.

"Hi ho, hi ho, it's off to work we go." Chang whistled in my ear as we started off under our heavy loads of gear.

He was just off my left shoulder, his gun raised, watching out for me so I could focus on Loki. If Loki's behavior changed, if he picked up a scent or heard something unusual, it could be our only warning before a bomb went off or the enemy attacked. My heart was pounding so hard in my chest, I couldn't believe my gun wasn't bouncing with every heartbeat.

I scanned the rocky terrain in front of me, my eyes darting to Loki and back to the surrounding boulders with every step.

Douglass walked about ten feet behind me and Chang, carrying the big M240 across his shoulders. The M240 was a massive belt-fed machine gun that must have weighed twenty-five pounds. I couldn't believe he could haul it all over these mountains in addition to the rest of his gear. We each had about fifty pounds strapped to our bodies between our packs and ammo and body armor and water, but the way Douglass moved, you would have thought he wasn't carrying a thing.

Lieutenant Schu was a few feet behind Douglass, fourth in the line, so he could keep his eye on me on my first combat patrol, but also so he could communicate with the rest of the platoon staggered out in a line behind him.

The platoon sergeant, a foul-mouthed Texan named Gaffley, checked in with each of us as we made our way through the maze of sandbags, past the razor wire, and down the rocky slope to a footpath along the ridge. Every other word he said was a curse, but he had a reassuring nod for every marine as he passed him, before he fell into the rear of the line.

With all the different sergeants and noncommissioned officers and the lieutenant, I felt like I had about a million different bosses. It was like a chart at the beginning of one of Zach's fantasy books, with all the elf kings and dukes and counts and princes listed, where you kept having to flip back to figure out who was who and how they were connected and which elf was really in charge.

In Afghanistan, I didn't have a chart like that. I just had to figure that everyone but me was in charge. Even Loki. I wasn't the lowest ranked, technically — that'd be the privates — but I was the least experienced. In the kingdom of elves, that made me a gnome, I guess. In Afghanistan, it just made me grateful to have the other marines watching my back.

The plan that first morning was to take the footpath along the spine of the mountains, down to the river valley, and check in with the elders in the nearest village. The lieutenant wanted to ask them what they knew about enemy fighters passing through the area, hiding weapons and planting bombs. He wanted Loki and me to search a few houses to see if we couldn't turn up some of those weapons.

Of course, we had to make it to the village first, and the footpath was a great place for the enemy to ambush us. There were boulders and scrubby trees at the edge of the path, crumbling stone walls were scattered here and there, and trenches for water runoff stretched alongside the route. Every few feet I'd think about where I'd take cover if we were attacked. There were a lot of good places to duck, and I comforted myself by picking out new ones as I walked.

Loki snuffled at the ground, his ears cocked, his eyes wide. He strained against the leash, eager to get to work.

"Over the river and through the woods," Chang sang quietly.

"Chang!" Douglass whisper-shouted from behind. "This ain't karaoke night at the Starlight Lounge. Quiet."

"Roger that," he answered and winked at me. "I just love driving Douglass crazy," he whispered.

"He's not the only one," I muttered back.

"Ooh, you got some fight in you yet," Chang chuckled. "I just might try to keep you from getting killed today after all."

"Thanks," I grumbled, and we walked on in silence. The air around us was cool, but starting to warm as the sun came up. That was the cruelty of where they'd built Outpost Eliopulos. At night it dipped below freezing. During the day, the area fried. It didn't seem like a place fit for people to live, but people had been living there for thousands of years. Some of the crumbling walls along the footpath looked like they might actually be thousands of years old. This was an old country, and it had been at war for a very long time. Even Alexander the Great couldn't conquer it. I wondered if his soldiers had walked along this same path.

It was amazing how my brain worked. I was terrified; I was on high alert for any sign of the enemy or for any change of behavior in Loki, but still, random thoughts kept coming to me. I remembered seeing Afghanistan on the colorful world map in my elementary school. It was just a pink blob in South Asia. At the time, I never could have imagined I'd be walking along its footpaths, a gun at my chest, a dog at my side, and a platoon of marines strung out behind me on the downward slope of a mountain littered with ancient ruins.

There were also more modern ruins along the footpath.

As we rounded a bend, we came upon the rusty shell of a burned-out Russian helicopter that had been shot down over twenty years ago. Loki sniffed at it, and, not caring about the history of the Russian invasion of this country, lifted his leg and peed on the wreck, marking his territory: Loki was here.

He sniffed at the road from side to side, his nose working overtime on all the smells. We walked that way for hours, no one talking. Lieutenant Schumacher would occasionally stop the line and we'd crouch, pointing our guns all around, listening. I'd pull Loki in to heel whenever that happened. It was so quiet, I wondered if everyone else could hear my heart beating as loud as thunder.

"Screeeeech!" A high-pitched whine cut the silence.

"Incoming!" Chang yelled, and all the marines dove to the side, pressing their faces into the dirt to take cover from what sounded like a heavy mortar shell streaking in. Mortars were like giant bullets that got launched high into the air and then arced down to the ground, exploding on impact. They could tear through walls and ceilings, and when they blew up, shards of hot metal flew out in all directions.

I felt totally exposed, fragile, even in my body armor with an M16 cradled against my chest. I dove into the trench along the side of the footpath, dragging Loki with me. Without thinking, running on instinct and training, I covered him with my body.

The whistle stopped and started again. Everyone waited. No explosion came. Chang stuck his head up, looking around.

"Do we have contact?" Lieutenant Schumacher asked.

Contact. That's elf talk for a gunfight. It made it sound more like dancing than like two groups of people trying to kill each other.

Chang was still looking around, scanning the trees around us, looking off to the mountains in the distance.

Another screech cut the air. Chang ducked again.

"Chang! Are we taking indirect fire or not?" Lieutenant Schumacher demanded. Indirect fire was elf speak for things like mortar attacks, where the enemy didn't have to be able to see us to hurt us. They could simply shoot mortar shells into the air and hope they'd drop on us from the sky.

"I don't know, sir!" Chang called back. We all flinched at another screech in the air. "It sure sounds like it."

But there were no explosions.

That's when Loki started barking and squirming underneath me.

"It's okay, boy." I tried to calm him. I worried he was freaking out. Combat stress. I thought about what Gunny had told me about losing control of my dog downrange. It could be a disaster, especially on my first patrol. "Calm down. Shhh. Calm down, boy."

But he didn't calm down. He barked like mad and wriggled out from under me, his nose pointing to the trees. This wasn't like him. This wasn't normal. Was he trying to tell me something? I followed his gaze to the tree and saw a small gray monkey perched on a branch, watching us.

"Screeech!" the monkey called.

"Screeech!" another monkey answered.

"It's monkeys!" I called. "Up there!" I pointed.

Everyone stood.

"Nice call, Chang," Lieutenant Schumacher said sarcastically. He gave the signal to keep moving.

"Every single time," Chang muttered as we started walking again, Loki keeping his eyes on the monkeys in the tree as we passed under it. "They always get me. I swear, the monkeys know it, man. They know they sound just like incoming mortars. They do it to mess with me."

"This has happened before?" I asked.

"I mean, why do they pick on me? I think they don't like Koreans. Racist monkeys. Messing with my head."

"Uh-huh," I grunted.

I felt strangely disappointed. I'd still never been in a firefight, and I didn't know how I'd do in one. The anticipation was worse than fear. It was the unknown that bothered me, and I was no closer to knowing than I'd been an hour ago. We kept marching.

"One of these days, I'm going monkey hunting," Chang grumbled as we walked. "I'm gonna make a hat out of those furry tree monsters. And a blanket. Maybe a toy for Loki."

I guess Chang really hated monkeys.

We hiked for another two hours. The sun had come up and was beating down on us. We'd crossed the mountain and gone down to the flat land at the edge of a dried-up river. A few irrigation ditches ran with meltwater from the snow of the mountains, and the mud around the ditches was a rich, dark brown. Everywhere else I looked was a reddish-yellow dusty color, even the low stone buildings of the village that were carved directly into the mountainside. They were built on top of each other up the slope, so that one family's roof was another's front yard.

As we approached the village, a young boy with a small herd of goats watched us carefully. He wore a long gray tunic and gray pants that looked like pajamas. He had on a little pillbox hat, and his hands clutched a thin stick that he used to whack the goats.

Loki immediately charged at the herd, and I pulled his leash short. The boy jumped backward, but when he saw me holding the dog back, he broke out into a smile. Loki lifted his front paw and cocked his head sideways at the boy. The boy imitated him, cocking his head to the side in the same way, and laughed.

I gave him a thumbs-up.

He smiled and gave me a thumbs-up right back. He made a motion, bringing his hand to his mouth and rubbing his stomach.

"What's he want?" I asked Chang.

"Candy," said Chang. "You give 'em candy once, and they never let you forget it." Chang dug in his pocket and tossed the boy a stick of gum. The boy caught it and gave Chang a thumbs-up.

Loki growled, and the boy's smile vanished. He turned and ran, the goats ambling after him. I noticed Chang had his finger on the trigger of his gun as the boy left.

"Seriously?" I said.

The boy had looked about the same age as my brother, Zach.

Chang shrugged. "Maybe I don't trust goats. In league with the monkeys."

As we walked into town, women covered in veils from head to toe scattered, vanishing behind closed doors. Old men with their beards dyed rusty orange watched us through hazy eyes. Little boys ran up and down along the sides of the path, calling to one another and pointing at Loki. It seemed strange that everyone was either an old man or a young boy. Where was everybody else?

"You see any cell phones come out, you interdict that individual," said Lieutenant Schumacher.

"Interdict?" Chang chuckled. "You don't gotta show off your SAT words all the time, sir."

"We can't all get by on our good looks like you, Chang," the lieutenant told him. "Just grab anyone you see pull out a cell phone."

"Aye-aye, Skipper," said Chang.

"Dempsey." Lieutenant Schumacher turned to me. "I want you to go ahead into that second house and search it with Loki. First squad will pull security for you."

"Yes, sir," I said, glad to have a job.

"Second squad, perimeter," said the lieutenant. "Third squad with me."

About twelve guys peeled off with Lieutenant Schu and went up to start talking to some of the old men. The lieutenant wanted to see what we could learn and how we might help the village. It was all part of trying to win over the hearts and minds of the local population . . . so that they wouldn't try to kill us.

We stepped up to the wooden door of the house, and Chang pounded on it. A younger man with a heavy black beard opened the door. Our unit translator came forward and chatted with him. They had a quick back and forth. It seemed like they were arguing about something.

"He says he has no weapons here," the translator told us.

"Well, tell him we've got to search anyway," Chang said. "Tell him we're coming in the easy way or the hard way."

The translator spoke again, and the man sighed and opened the door.

Four marines whose names I didn't remember went in to round up all the people inside and clear them out of Loki's way. Sergeant Gaffley stood with the rest of the squad, watching the street, although I knew he had one eye on me. A crowd had gathered around us, some of them talking to the translator, who told them to step back.

"Clear!" we heard the guys call from inside after a few minutes.

Chang nodded at me.

"Okay, Loki." I bent down to my dog's face. "Here we go, buddy."

It was time to get to work.

CHAPTER 10

CHOICES

Loki's tail spun like a helicopter blade. His snout rose in the air. He could sense that something was about to happen. Even though this was new to me, Loki had done this before.

I pulled his toy from my pocket. He immediately perked his ears up and hopped from foot to foot. His tail stopped wagging and pointed, ready for action. I slipped the toy back into my pocket, so he knew he'd only get it as a reward for finding what he'd been trained to find.

For Loki, the game had begun.

I glanced at the crowd on the street around us. Chang and the others on the squad were watching them closely. A mixture of faces, young and old, now all had their eyes fixed on me. For some of them, it was just curiosity about the

American and his dog. But there were probably some who were watching my every move as spies. I felt very exposed on that street and was grateful for Chang by my side.

I took a deep breath.

"Seek, seek," I commanded, unclipping Loki's leash from his thick leather collar and pointing him toward the house. He bolted away, through the open doorway and into the shadows, snuffling and sniffing in every corner. I followed with Chang right behind me. I had to stay close, encouraging Loki and pointing, telling him where to focus his attention, all my senses on high alert. The place could be booby-trapped.

It was a one-room house, with a carpet hanging toward the back to separate the cooking area from the rest of it. There was one bed, and a lot of rugs and mats rolled in the corners. A small door led to a terrace, and there was a single window, filled right now with the faces of curious boys, eager to see an American dog team at work.

Loki was gulping in air through his nostrils, a loud nasal snort that sucked in all kinds of smells. They say a human nose has about six million smell receptors. A Labrador retriever has around 150 million of them. Humans usually only notice smells that are good or bad, but a dog smells the way humans see colors, with different shades and hues and brightnesses.

They can smell objects and the different people who have touched those objects. They can smell moods, like fear, and they can even tell time with their sense of smell — how long it's been since a smell showed up, how quickly it's fading. Loki was trained to smell explosives and weapons, but his nose could also pick up on places where explosives or weapons had been.

I had to watch him closely. If he picked up something on a blanket, it could mean that the blanket had been wrapped around guns or bomb parts, and that could mean the owner of the blanket might know something about the bad guys, might even be working with them. That also meant that if Loki picked up on something and the owner noticed, the owner might attack us.

Loki crawled under the bed. He sniffed at a rolled rug. He pawed through the drawers of a dresser, sniffing at the clean clothes. The whole time, the owner of the house stood on his tiptoes at the edge of the room, watching over Chang's shoulder and yelling. I couldn't understand his words, but he was obviously objecting to the dog crawling all over his stuff. If I were him, I'd be angry too . . . Loki's paws were filthy.

But his shouting was making me nervous. I didn't want him watching my dog work.

"Get him out of here," I told Chang.

Chang and the translator started to move the man out of the room, just as Loki and I got to a bin filled with vegetable scraps and bits of bone. It was some sort of composting bin, but it was weird that they'd keep it in the house. Even I could smell it without a powerful dog nose. Who would want to live with that smell?

Loki started to act funny. He sniffed around the edge of the bin and then paced back and forth in front of it. He looked back at me. I knew the look from training. It said, *Hey, boss, I think I might be on to something here.*

He stood on his back legs, his paws on the lid of the bin, and took in big snorts of air, checking and double-checking what his nose was trying to tell him. Then he paced back and forth again and sat right in front of the bin, alert and still. That was his way of telling me he was sure. He'd found something.

The owner of the house was really shouting now, waving his arms in the air.

Chang pressed him against the wall and ordered him to stay still and stay quiet. I approached the bin slowly and flipped the lid open. The stench of rotting vegetables and the sour smell of old meat almost overwhelmed me. I worried Loki had picked up a false scent or was just saying he wanted some of that meat. Just because he'd found *something* didn't mean he'd found what we were looking for. Only I could confirm that.

I pulled out my utility knife and sorted through the disgusting heap of garbage. I pushed down into it until my wrist was covered in filth. Then my elbow. I heard Loki let out a whimper, eager to know if he'd done well. Eager to get his prize.

My heart raced, hoping to find something, terrified I'd find something.

I reached deeper, all the way to the bottom of the bin, and my knife clanged on a hard object — a plastic tube.

"We've got something!" I shouted, and Chang passed the message outside. Some of the other marines came over to unload the bin. They pulled out wires and a sack of ammonium nitrate . . . all the ingredients to make an improvised explosive device. An IED.

"These yours?" Chang yelled at the owner of the house. "These belong to you? Huh? You trying to hurt marines with these?"

We didn't need the translator to know the man was trying to deny it, to make excuses. The tone of his voice was just like that of a kid in trouble at school for something he knows he did, but didn't think he'd get caught at. Someone went to get the lieutenant.

I turned to Loki.

"That's a good boy!" I praised him.

The bad guys were smart. They weren't using any metal in their bomb parts so that our metal detectors wouldn't pick up on it. They hid the pieces in a disgusting bin of rotting food, figuring we wouldn't go poking around in the garbage.

But they didn't count on Loki and his amazing nose.

I pulled his toy out and tossed it straight up. He leaped and snatched it from the air and snorted with glee, prancing around in circles with the toy in his mouth. He knew he'd done a good job, and he loved showing off. That was probably a bad habit too, but I let it slide. He'd just given us a success our first time out. I smiled watching him.

Lieutenant Schu came in with a few of the village elders trailing behind him. Our translator spoke rapidly, repeating in English what they were saying in their Pashto language.

"He's a good man," they were saying.

"Fighters make him hide things here or they kill his wife, his children," they were saying.

"He had no choice," they were saying.

"Tell them that there is always a choice," Lieutenant Schumacher told the translator. He turned to the elders and spoke slowly so that the translator would have time to repeat what he said accurately. "If you have a problem with fighters coming here and hiding things in your homes, you tell me. You know where to find me. The base is right up on the hill. You come tell me that fighters are threatening you, trying to use your village to hide their weapons, and I'll come after them and they will regret it. My marines and I are here to protect you. But you keep secrets from me, you make me come here with my dog and find this stuff — this stuff they use to hurt and to kill my marines — well, then I think you've made a choice. You've made a bad choice, and I can't help you if you're going to make bad choices."

When the translator finished, the elders shook their heads and spat on the ground. They didn't like what they were hearing. I guess they also didn't like hearing it from a guy who was less than half their age. He didn't even have a beard. None of us did. We were clean-shaven Americans. In their culture, all the grown men had beards. So it must have been doubly humiliating because Lieutenant Schumacher looked like a boy to them, and yet he had a fully armed marine platoon and the might of the United States Military to back him up. They couldn't so easily dismiss what he said as childish.

"Now I'm gonna take this man to answer some questions," the lieutenant explained, pointing at the owner of the house, who was kneeling on the floor with his hands behind his head, while Chang stood above him with his M16. "He'll be treated fairly. We're not going to hurt him, but he is going to come with us now, understood?"

Whether the elders understood or not, it didn't really matter. The lieutenant nodded, and a marine tied the man's hands behind his back with a tight plastic band, then put a blindfold on him. Standard operating procedure for arresting a suspected insurgent.

The lieutenant called in a helicopter to come get the man and take him to Camp Leatherneck, the biggest base in the region, where he would be sitting down with some military interrogators. What happened to the man after he got there was up to someone else, higher ranked officers than Lieutenant Schumacher. We were the knights in the field. Big decisions were made by kings back in the castle.

"He says he had no choice." The translator repeated the man's pleas in English as we waited for the helicopter to come get him. The rest of the platoon were standing around, watching the crowd.

"Nice work, Dempsey," Sergeant Gaffley said, although he said it with more four letter words than that. "*Hajji* take-down number one."

Hajji was a term of honor for a Muslim who had made a pilgrimage to the Muslim holy places, but Sergeant Gaffley didn't mean it as a compliment. He called all the locals *hajji* even though we'd been told in basic training that using the word that way was an insult. I guess it was easier for him to call them names than to see them as real people, especially when some of them were trying to kill us. Sergeant Gaffley had been in Afghanistan a lot longer than I had.

I suddenly felt a knot in my stomach. My pride left a chalky taste in my mouth. The man was being taken away because of me and Loki. I started to wonder . . . What if he was telling the truth? What choice did he have if the terrorists had really threatened his family?

But what choice did we have either?

If we didn't take that stuff, it'd be turned into a bomb and probably used against us. We'd all end up like Loki's last handler. And maybe the man was lying. Maybe he was working with the bad guys of his own free will. Maybe he'd even fired the shot that had killed Corporal Eliopulos.

That's what war was. A series of bad choices, one worse than the next, and from the moment a war starts they fall like dominoes. Fighters came into this area, so the marines came into this area. Fighters used the village to hide, so the marines searched the village. Fighters shot at the marines, so the marines shot back. Innocent, guilty, for or against the war . . . It didn't really matter.

The dominoes were already falling when we got here.

I envied Loki. For him it was all play. He did what he'd been trained to do without question, and he enjoyed it. I decided then and there to take the same approach. Find the weapons, stop the bombs, protect my marines. I'd let the officers and the politicians worry about the rest of it. If I looked too far past the end of my leash, I'd lose my mind.

"You did good work today," Lieutenant Schu said. He put his hand on my shoulder and looked me right in the eyes, like he could see the chaos in my brain at that moment. "I hope you know that. Finding that stuff probably saved lives, understood?"

"Oo-rah," I said quietly, and scratched Loki behind his ears.

Once the helicopter lifted off again, in a swirl of noise and dust, the lieutenant had us move out of the village. It was late afternoon and he wanted to get back to base before dusk, when the long shadows on the mountains gave the bad guys more places to hide and wait in ambush.

"Dempsey, you and Loki take point again," he ordered.

"Aye-aye, sir," I said, feeling good about our success as a team and ready to keep showing what we could do.

"We're gonna get hit," Chang said as we started the march. "I can feel it. The whole valley knows we're here and they know where we're going. They'd be crazy *not* to attack us."

"Just keep your mouth shut and your eyes open," Douglass said, cradling his heavy machine gun in his arms. "Like Dempsey and Loki."

I smiled. I guess being good at the job was more important than being the most fun guy in the platoon. I was starting to like Douglass.

"Will you scratch behind my ears if I do?" Chang joked.

"I'll put you on a leash," Douglass replied.

Their back-and-forth banter went on for a while as we made our way through the irrigation ditches to the footpath that led up the mountain. I found the banter calming. It was like the chatter in the locker room in high school. It made it feel almost like we were just some normal guys going for a walk after gym class.

We passed the spot where Loki had scared off the boy and his goats. The tops of the mountains on the other side of the valley were shrouded in mist. Our own mountain sloped up in front of us, the afternoon haze hiding the outpost from our view. It was nice to know they were up there somewhere, watching over us with their heavy artillery, ready to help out if we got into trouble.

Loki snuffled at the last ditch before the climb up. It was filled with wastewater and goat droppings and mud. He put his nose right down above it, just a hair's width away from its oily surface, snorting in all those smells. I wrinkled my nose and fought my gag reflex, but I guess for Loki, sniffing a wastewater ditch was like reading a really interesting book filled with information about the whole area — what people ate, what they planted, who they were, and when they'd been there.

All I smelled was goat poop.

And maybe some from humans too.

I pulled Loki along, forcing him to pick up his pace. "Come on, boy," I urged. I wanted to get away from the gross smell and I wanted to get back to base. I was tired from almost no sleep and a long hike and a hard search, and we still had a long way to go.

Loki looked at me with wide eyes and a look that I can only describe as hangdog. He was upset I was ruining his good time. I nudged him forward, and he trotted ahead of me with a sigh.

Then he stopped. He sniffed at the air, frozen. I saw his tail tighten, his behavior change, like he'd picked up on a smell he knew. I raised my arm, signaling for the column of marines behind me to stop, just in case.

And that's when the world around us exploded.

CHAPTER 11

CONTACT

"Contact, contact, contact!" Chang shouted.

I heard a *snap* as a firefly zipped past my face.

The dirt started dancing at my feet.

"Get down!" Chang pulled me into the waste ditch we'd just crossed over. I skittered down the dirt embankment and sank up to my knees in the foul water, pulling Loki in behind me. More fireflies buzzed overhead.

It took me another fraction of a second to realize they were tracer rounds from our guns returning fire. The "firefly" I'd seen before was an enemy bullet buzzing past my helmet. I was in my first firefight.

Contact.

I pressed Loki against the dirt as I lifted my head to see where the shots were coming from. I was curious. It was a strange emotion to feel, but I'd never been shot at before. Mud kicked up just in front of my face, and I ducked down again.

"They're shooting at us!" I yelled.

"Duh!" Chang yelled back over the roar of the gunfire. To my other side, Douglass had set the M240 on its tripod in the mud and opened fire. The barrel was smoking, hot brass casings ejecting into the filthy water around us. He had a grin on his face as his shoulder rattled with the force of the gun unloading on fully-automatic.

Chang popped up over the top of the ditch and fired a few rounds from his M16 before ducking back down next to me.

I wanted to get up and fire back, to do something, but I also had to keep Loki safe. He was half in the dirty water and half out, his face pressed down flat on his paws. He was looking up at me, waiting patiently for me to make all the noise and smoky smells stop.

I wished I'd put on his special dog body armor. I had worried about Loki overheating or tiring out too soon on his first patrol in months. Now I worried about a bullet tearing him apart because I hadn't put his armor on him. I had my armor on, though, and I decided to stay above Loki, covering him with my body . . . just like Corporal Eliopulos had.

I popped over the top of the ditch, pointing my gun at the sloping mountain in front of us.

I didn't even know where to aim. The air was thick with black smoke from the explosion of the IED that had started the firefight. I guess it went off too early to get any of us. Maybe the bad guys got nervous seeing Loki and didn't want him to find it before they could blow it. Maybe they just got clumsy and pressed the button too soon. Whatever happened, I was glad to be alive, my heart pounding, my focus intense, and adrenaline racing through my body. I wasn't afraid. Things were happening too fast to feel afraid. Fear came before, and maybe it would come after. But right at that moment, I just felt like doing something.

They were trying to kill Chang with his quick comebacks and Douglass and foul-mouthed Sergeant Gaffley and Lieutenant Schumacher, and all those guys whose names I hadn't even had a chance to learn yet. I couldn't let that happen.

I pointed my weapon where everyone else seemed to be shooting and I squeezed the trigger.

I'd never shot a weapon at another human being before. The gun bucked a little in my hands and the bullets flew out and the shells ejected and my shots crackled against the hillside. I knew I hadn't hit anything other than dirt, and I surprised myself by cursing. At that moment, I *wanted* to hurt the people who were trying to hurt us. I *wanted* to hit something other than dirt. At the same time, I was relieved I hadn't.

Two totally opposite emotions, churning inside me.

I ducked back down to comfort Loki, who was shaking now. "Good boy," I said to him. "You're okay, good boy. It's all okay."

I wondered if Eliopulos had told him the same thing when they came under fire together the last time. I wonder if Loki believed it. Dogs know when something is wrong. They can smell it.

"This is Echo-One Actual," Lieutenant Schumacher was calling into the radio. "I've got a TIC at position Homer."

TIC meant troops in contact, and position Homer was the code name for the place where the path back to the outpost met the flatland on the way to the village. Its code name changed all the time, in case the enemy was listening. Today it was named for a character from the Simpsons. Tomorrow it might be a sports team.

He pulled out a map, studying it quickly, and shouted some coordinates to the artillery team at one of the bases across the valley. The mountains were dotted with bases and outposts like ours so that they could support one another. If one came under an attack it couldn't repel, another could aim its big guns that way and clean up the mess.

We all waited a moment and then heard the shriek of heavy artillery rounds fly over us, pounding into the side of the mountain. The ground rumbled. The dirty water in the irrigation ditch shook. The shriek of the artillery and the explosions on impact were like the biggest, baddest fireworks show I'd ever seen — more like a wizard's festival from one of Zach's fantasy books than an average Fourth of July. I couldn't believe it, but I felt a smile burst onto my face in the middle of it all. I hadn't thought war was supposed to be fun.

When the dust and smoke cleared, the air smelled heavily of gunpowder, but it was quiet.

Second squad, led by Sergeant Gaffley in front, moved forward to investigate while we covered them from below. Once they gave us the all clear, we finally crawled out of the ditch.

"Another job well done, dog team," Lieutenant Schumacher told me as we started up again. "A few more steps forward and I would have been writing some letters home to grieving parents."

"Yes, sir," I said.

"Loki okay to take point again?"

I looked down at Loki, who was panting and sniffing around happily, the firefight already a distant memory, the disgusting wastewater smells all over the marines' pants legs much more interesting now.

"Good to go, sir," I told him.

"Roger that. Let's move."

Chang, Loki, and I moved ahead to catch up with the second squad.

"Thanks for pulling me down back there," I told Chang.

"I had to," he said. "I've got a bet with Douglass. You can't get killed until you laugh at one of my jokes."

"Then I'm gonna live a long life," I told him.

We got quiet when we reached the second squad. They were standing around the burned landscape, which was pocked with bullet holes. Where once there had been a stand of trees and a low stone wall, there was nothing but smoking heaps of ash. It was like the surface of the moon.

One of the second-squad marines — De La Peña, his name patch said — nodded and hitched his thumb at one smoking heap. At first I didn't know what I was looking at. Then I saw the burned-up pillbox hat, a streak of gray in the pajamas. And the shining silver foil of a stick of gum.

The shepherd boy.

There were two men nearby, both on the ground face down, their clothes and hair burned, their bodies torn apart, weapons melted and mangled in the dirt beside them.

But I couldn't take my eyes off the boy.

The platoon corpsman — a navy medic who served with the marines — was bent over the charred pile of flesh that had been a boy just a few hours ago. He was checking for vital signs, a heartbeat, breath, anything . . . but he stood up, shaking his head.

"Just a kid," he sighed, scratching the back of his neck. "Vasquez," he introduced himself to me. Loki wagged his tail. "Glad you brought Loki back to us."

"Uh, yeah," I said, feeling strange about making small talk on the edge of this scorched hillside, surrounded by bodies.

"Looks like the rest of them scampered off," De La Peña said. "Probably hightailed it up over the back of the ridge when the big guns opened up on them."

"Do we pursue?" I asked, thinking about Loki's powerful nose. "They can't have gone far."

"Go after them?" Sergeant Gaffley shook his head. "*Hajji*'s got caves all over the place. They ditch their weapons and pretend to be shepherds. We'd never find them."

"But Loki . . ." I started. He wasn't really trained to track people, just bombs and guns, but still, he was a Labrador retriever. Tracking was in his blood.

I wanted to go after the bad guys. I was angry. Not only did they try to kill us, but they'd used that boy, that boy the same age as my brother. They'd poisoned his brain and given him a gun and put him right in our way.

They had to know what would happen.

His blood was on their hands.

Not mine.

But I'd fired. I'd fired into the hills just like everyone else.

But I'd missed.

But I hadn't wanted to miss.

"Come on, John Wayne," Chang nudged me forward. "We'll go hunting fugitives another day."

As we stepped out ahead of second squad to lead the way back to OPE, I looked back at the burned body of the shepherd boy.

No choice at all, I thought.

Loki walked ahead, sniffing the road from side to side, and I followed him up the mountain, the line of marines falling in behind us.

I kept my eyes on my dog and didn't look back.

123

ABOUT POOP

Poop.

There's no way to avoid it.

Life as a dog handler at a military outpost in a combat zone means a lot of poop.

The outpost was a collection of tight spaces where guys walked around barefoot and there were weapons everywhere and sometimes we had to scramble if it looked like an attack was coming in. No one wanted to step in dog poop, so I spent a lot of time wandering around, making sure Loki didn't leave behind any surprises.

At Combat Outpost Eliopulos, the marines didn't have anyone to clean up after us. We did our own cleaning, with water that was brought in by locals from the rivers in the mountains. We washed our own clothes when we had to. (Like right after the firefight in the drainage ditch. The other two platoons made us clean up before we stank up the whole outpost . . . at least, worse than it already stank.) We also had to gather up all our garbage and burn it every few days.

That included Loki's poop.

But not just *Loki's* poop.

We didn't have any running water at the outpost. When we needed to use the head — marine elf speak for toilet — we had four open stalls, each with a wooden seat positioned above a metal bucket. The stalls had no doors, but a nice view of the mountains. There were no women around, and we all lived so closely that there wasn't much need for privacy. Anyway, the Marine Corps didn't really *do* privacy. We got to know each other whether we wanted to or not. For example, I quickly learned that Chang liked to rap while he sat on the head.

Lucky Chang's the name, how can I deny it?
I got more rhymes than LA's got diets.
I bust my caps up at OPE,
Shoot up the 'Stan with my M16.
Break it down for me, O.G. Low-Key!

That's usually when Loki would bark. I don't know how Chang trained him to do it, or why Corporal Eliopulos let him, but it made going to the bathroom entertaining.

The steel buckets under the seats collected our business, and every other day, we'd gather it all, pour some fuel onto it, and burn it so it didn't stink up the place. The burning job rotated among the enlisted men of Echo Company, and no one ever wanted it, which meant I got to do it for my first three weeks.

I was the new guy.

Those were the rules.

"It's the law of fecal gravity," Douglass explained.

I didn't know what he meant.

"You know . . . fecal. Feces?" He shook his head. "Like, what's in the buckets? And gravity. It means that stuff rolls downhill. You're the new guy, the noob, so the dirtiest job rolls down to you."

The other guys all agreed. I had to obey the rule of fecal gravity.

When I wasn't cleaning up or burning buckets of poop or taking up a post and watching the valley from a bunker with Loki sleeping at my feet, he and I were training.

I'd hide samples of bomb-making stuff around the

outpost and show Loki his toy, and he'd go off and find what I'd hidden. The other guys loved to watch, to see what he could do. They all offered to help by hiding the samples for me, usually in one another's stuff.

Especially in Chang's stuff.

He'd come back from a shift on watch or from working out or cleaning up or rapping on the toilet, excited to lay down and sleep for a few hours, and he'd find that a dog had torn his rack apart, unpacked his bag, and drooled all over his one clean shirt. Loki loved rolling around on anything clean. He liked to get rid of the clean smells as quickly as possible, I guess, make everything smell like him, like it should. Luckily for him, clean smells were rare up at OPE.

Loki had memorized the smells of all the other marines in Echo Company, and he was very protective. Whenever locals would come with the water, he'd growl and watch them suspiciously. Whenever someone would come from the village to tell us news or speak to the lieutenant about a problem, Loki sniffed them first to make sure they didn't have any hidden explosives strapped to their bodies, and then he usually growled anyway.

He knew he was a marine and he didn't trust anyone who wasn't.

The days went by. Most of the time things were pretty dull. We'd go for patrols, hearts pounding, nerves tingling, and we'd all feel a bit let down when nothing happened. And we'd all feel a bit relieved too. Always the opposite feelings at the same time. That's how war worked.

On one patrol, Loki found an old Russian mortar shell. On another, he went crazy when he found a kitchen timer buried by a burned tree stump.

"Why'd he smell this?" I asked Chang.

"They hook these kitchen timers up to a mortar cannon and then run away. The cannon fires when the timer goes off, and the bad guys are long gone by then. We can't return fire. There's no one to hit. This one must have gotten some of that smell on it. Must have been used."

"So we're at war with kitchen timers?"

"Roger that," Chang laughed. "Cell phones, kitchen timers. Even our own self-heating MREs."

"The meals ready to eat?" I couldn't imagine how those could be turned into weapons. The military already made us eat the disgusting things.

"They can be turned into booby traps," Chang explained. "The heating packet can be rigged to explode and snap your ankles. Probably hurt Loki pretty bad because he's closer to the ground."

I looked at Loki lifting his leg to mark the stump, his soft underbelly exposed. He could be killed by an enemy we'd never even see: a buried bomb hooked up to a cell phone, a rocket set off by a kitchen timer.

I shut those thoughts out. We had a job to do. I kept the kitchen timer to use in training. He'd have to learn what they smelled like too.

One morning, I was sitting outside in the shade of the netting, leaning on some sandbags and brushing Loki. Douglass and Doc Vasquez came over in the middle of a conversation.

"I am telling you, Doc," Douglass said, loud enough to make sure I heard it. "Dempsey does not let anybody play with his dog. I mean, *he* doesn't even play with his dog except for training. He's too gung ho for all that."

"Nobody is that gung ho," Doc Vasquez said and glanced at me.

It sounded like they'd rehearsed their little "chat" and were performing it now for my benefit — and overacting too.

I thought about explaining how training *was* playing, but Loki had sniffed them coming over and was looking up at them, panting and wagging his tail. He turned to me, his dark eyes begging.

I was about to tell the guys that I had to finish grooming him, and then we could do some training together if they wanted. But now they were all three staring at me with big puppy dog eyes. Vasquez had even taken off his sunglasses to make sure I got the point.

"Pretty please?" Vasquez said.

Loki let out one low whimper and shifted his weight from paw to paw. He was doing his cute act.

Bad habits, I thought. But I let go of his collar and nodded. It was enough of a cue for Loki. He twisted around and dove right onto Vasquez, licking his face like an ice cream cone. Vasquez rolled him, and Loki dove out of his grip — he wasn't about to let *another* human put him on his back. In one quick move he snatched Vasquez's sunglasses out of his hand, gripping them loosely in his mouth and slobbering all over them.

Vasquez reached to grab them back, and Loki leaped just out of reach. Vasquez scrambled toward him, and Loki leaped in the other direction.

"Come on, Loki, give me those!" he pleaded. Loki

snorted, Vasquez lunged, and Loki bolted in the other direction, Vasquez laughing in pursuit, racing through the maze of the base, up the slopes, through the twisting rows of HESCOs and bunkers.

"You believe he wants to be a doctor?" Douglass muttered, watching them run off. "Man can't even keep his glasses from a dog."

Watching them run, it struck me that I didn't know much about Vasquez, except that he was from somewhere in Wyoming, listened to the worst heavy metal I had ever heard, and that the MRE spaghetti and meatballs didn't agree with his stomach.

After the incident with the shepherd boy, we had stood next to each other to wash our pants. Mine were covered in muck and filth from the drainage ditch. His were streaked with blood from the boy. We didn't talk, and at the time I appreciated it. I was still buzzing from my first combat. I hadn't even wondered about what was in his head, the medic with the gun, the wannabe doctor covered in the blood of a shepherd boy we'd killed.

I could hear him uphill, calling Loki's name, pleading for his sunglasses back. I knew how hard Loki could be to catch when he didn't want to be caught.

I thought back to training and to Gunny. I thought about the baby talk with the ammo cans, and Harry Potter, and the zerbert he gave me. Gunny had been in the war and seen young guys just like me injured and dying, and he knew our whole training class would be going to war soon too.

Maybe he and Loki understood the same thing: You can't be tough all the time.

Sometimes you need to read a book about wizards. Sometimes you need to act like a goofball. Sometimes you just need to play.

"Listen up!" Staff Sergeant Luken came strutting down from the headquarters building.

He looked at me and Douglass, ran his eyes over the surrounding mess of empty energy drink cans and open MRE packets, the rifles lying around, the spent ammo littering the dirt, and he shook his head. "We need to get this place squared away. We've got Colonel Levithan coming in on a bird at thirteen hundred to give this place a once-over. I do not want him to see us living in our own —"

"I got him!" Doc Vasquez strutted back down the hill, interrupting the Staff Sergeant's rant. He held his sunglasses high, dripping with drool. Loki was at his heels, running in circles around him and leaping to try and snatch the glasses back. Vasquez kept having to turn and block Loki with his body. "O.G. Loki ain't so hardcore!"

"Vasquez! What the hell are you doing?" Luken shouted. "Can it! And Dempsey, get control of your dog! We're not running a doggy day care here."

My face flushed. The one time I let Loki cut loose, and I get yelled at.

"I want this place in shipshape," the staff sergeant yelled. "Vasquez, get those heads cleaned."

"But Dempsey's the new guy!" Vasquez objected. "He's on doodie duty."

Staff Sergeant Luken gave Vasquez a look that made it crystal clear to all of us it was now Vasquez's turn to clean the heads.

He shook his head. "Colonel's coming, so now I gotta scramble to clean toilets. It ain't right."

"Fecal gravity," nodded Douglass.

"Dempsey!" The staff sergeant turned to me. "You get Loki ready. When the Colonel gets here, Lieutenant Schu wants to do a demonstration for him of what our dog team can do."

"I'll need a volunteer to wear the bite sleeve," I said. I figured if we were going to do a demonstration, we'd do the full show, just like I'd done for the kids back in California. Except this time, I'd be the one calling the shots. I only had a protective sleeve with me, not the full suit, but that wouldn't matter. These were battle-tested marines, right?

"Don't look at me, bro." Vasquez shook his head. "I'm a lover, not a fighter."

"I don't do dog attacks," Douglass said.

"Don't even think it," the staff sergeant told me when I looked his way.

"*I just wanna be your dog . . . !*" Chang screeched out the lyrics to an old punk song as he came down the hill from a workout in his boxer shorts and sneakers, his dog tags shimmering in the afternoon sun and a toothbrush poking from his mouth.

Our heads swiveled toward him and he stopped in his tracks. Even Loki stared him down.

Staff Sergeant Luken nodded at me. "You've got your volunteer," he said.

"Uh . . ." Chang said, pulling out the toothbrush. "I miss something?"

"You stepped in it now, Chang," Douglass laughed, as I went off to find the bite sleeve, with Loki at my heels and Chang following close behind.

CHAPTER 13

FULL-BIRD

The colonel arrived an hour late because of bad weather. His chopper was barely on the ground for a minute before it took off again. If it stayed too long on the landing zone, the enemy might get a shot off at it. The helicopters cost millions of dollars, and the military did not want to risk damaging them when they didn't have to.

Chang and I were waiting down by the mess tent, the only area large enough to do our demonstration. Chang was telling me all about his little Chihuahua back in Los Angeles. He was nervous and, like a lot of guys, he babbled when he got nervous.

"My girlfriend named her Pixie." He shook his head. "Ex-girlfriend. My ex-girlfriend. But come on? Pixie? That's no name for a dog, even a little rat-looking dog like mine.

But names, you know, they stick to you, so she's Pixie now and Pixie forever. Like in the Corps. No one ever called me Chang before I joined the Corps. Everyone called me by my first name. It's Ben, by the way. I was always Ben or maybe Benny. But the second I joined the Corps, I lost my name. I was Recruit, then I was Private, and now I'm just Chang. It's like they want us to lose our identities."

"That *is* what they want," I told him. "We aren't supposed to be who we were as civilians. We're supposed to be more than who we were. We're marines. We're part of a brotherhood."

"You go for all that? Like calling me Ben will keep me from shooting straight?" Chang was plucking at the heavy bite sleeve around his arm, making sure it was secure for the fifth time. He was sitting on a pile of sandbags with his feet up, trying to look relaxed.

"Loyalty," I said. "That's the test of a real man. I believe in that. And that's what the Corps teaches us."

"Sure, yeah, *Semper Fi*," Chang said. "But I didn't sign up because I wanted to join the boy scouts. I just thought I'd look cool with an M16. I mean, I got your back because you got mine, not because some official code of conduct says so. And now, I've got to put on a show because some colonel is showing up. He's just a man. Out of the uniform he could be anyone, a greeter at Walmart or something." He worried at a snag on the bite sleeve with his fingers. "And why do they spell *colonel* like that? Shouldn't it be spelled like *kernel*, like a popcorn kernel?"

"Don't be nervous," I told him. "Loki won't hurt you. Not on purpose anyway."

"Who said I was nervous? I'm just talking, passing time. I'm not nervous. Nervous? What?"

"You're talking a lot, Chang. Even for you."

"Well someone has to! You don't say a word. You talk more to that dog than you do to people. I mean, I get that you like dogs, but man, how'm I supposed to be all *Semper Fi* when you won't even say nothing? Like, crack a joke sometime."

"Knock, knock," I told him.

He cocked his head at me and wrinkled his eyebrow. "You tellin' me a joke, Dempsey?"

"Knock, knock," I said again. Chang shook his head and smiled.

"A'ight. A'ight. I got you. Who's there?"

"Colonel Levithan."

"Colonel Levithan who?"

"Colonel Levithan, battalion commander. Behind you," I said, as the colonel and Lieutenant Schumacher came up the hill toward us. Chang looked back and fell off the sandbags in his hurry to stand. He pulled himself up, brushed himself off, and saluted the colonel. The silver eagle on Colonel Levithan's collar shined brightly, the mark of his rank (which is why colonels were sometimes called "full-bird colonels").

"As you were," the colonel said, looking instantly down at Loki, just like everyone did when they first saw him. He smiled. Everyone usually did that too. "And who's this marine?"

"Military Working Dog Loki and Corporal Gus Dempsey," Lieutenant Schumacher told him. "And this is Private Ben Chang. If you don't mind, sir, they're going to give you a little demonstration of what the dog teams can do. I hope it'll help you in thinking about deploying these teams effectively."

"Let's see it," the colonel nodded. Colonel Levithan was probably only in his forties, but Staff Sergeant Luken had been the oldest guy I'd seen for weeks, and he was only, like, thirty, so seeing Colonel Levithan made me feel like the grown-ups had suddenly shown up to ruin our fun. Playtime was over.

"Sir, we'll be demonstrating a basic takedown of a fleeing suspect and a simple search for common IED supplies," I explained. "Loki is a trained IED detector dog, so suspect interdiction is not his primary area of training."

"Slow down there, Corporal," the colonel said. "That's a lot of words you're firing off. Let's just see what your team can do, okay?"

"Yes, sir," I said, kicking myself for doing just what Chang had done. I guess I talked when I got nervous too. I didn't used to. But Loki made me nervous. I didn't know if I was going to get playful-goofball Loki or master-IED-detector-dog Loki.

I bent down and showed Loki his toy. He immediately perked his ears up, ready to work. "Seek, seek!" I commanded, and off he went, sniffing around the edges of the sandbags, circling supply boxes. After a few minutes, he paced back to one particular sandbag and then sat in front of it, looking back at me. I walked over, pulled out my knife, and sliced the bag open. I reached into the sand and pulled out the kitchen timer we'd found while on patrol.

"Good boy," I said, tossing Loki's toy for him. He ran off and fetched it, parading it around happily in front of the colonel and the lieutenant and the other marines who'd gathered to watch the show.

Now came the good part. I told Chang to climb up onto one of the high HESCO barriers, like he was a bad guy trying to get away. When he was halfway over, about to drop down the other side and out of sight, I pointed at him and shouted my command: "Get him! Go!"

Loki shot like a bullet, dropping his toy and racing across the clearing. He launched himself off the ground and caught Chang on the arm in midair, yanking him right off the barrier and into the dirt. Chang landed with a thud on his side, and Loki landed gracefully beside him, never losing his grip. He started to do his tug-of-war thing with Chang's arm.

"Get off me, get off! Ahh!" Chang play-acted, even though he was laughing as he said it. Some of the guys watching snapped pictures with their digital cameras.

"You gotta e-mail me some of those pics," I whispered to Douglass, while Chang squirmed and shouted on the ground.

"You kidding?" said Douglass. "I'm e-mailing these to *everyone*."

I nodded and then stepped forward. "Out, out!" I called and ran over to pull Loki off Chang. "Good boy!" I gave him a small treat and let him run off to chew on his toy. Then I turned back to the colonel.

"Very good, son," the colonel said.

"I can tell you from experience, sir, every patrol feels safer with Loki on it," Lieutenant Schu told the Colonel. "He and Corporal Dempsey are really cutting off the enemy at the knees."

"I'm sure of it," the colonel said.

"Thank you, sir," I nodded as Loki came back to sit beside me at attention.

"Keep up the good work, marines." The colonel bent down to give Loki a pat on the head.

I couldn't react in time.

Loki didn't know Colonel Levithan's smell and wasn't about to let some total stranger put hands on him. I'd learned that the hard way when I picked him up from the airport. Loki barked and bared his teeth and lunged at the colonel, catching the edge of his sleeve. He tugged and snarled, the hair on his back standing straight up, pure animal rage.

"Loki! Out!" I yelled as the colonel stumbled backward. I tugged Loki back by his leather collar and held him. He was up on his back legs, still barking and growling at the highest ranking officer I'd ever met. "Out!" I yelled again. "I'm so sorry, sir," I told the colonel. "He's a very friendly dog, but sometimes strangers make him nervous."

"Understood, Corporal," the colonel said. He was still backing away, rubbing his wrist where Loki's teeth had grazed him.

"That attitude makes Loki a very effective guard dog," the lieutenant explained, his eyes wide with panic, just like mine.

"Don't worry about it, Lieutenant Schumacher. It's my own fault for petting him without asking. He's a working dog, not some household pet. I guess I just miss my own dogs and forgot myself."

"Yes, sir," Lieutenant Schu and I said in unison. He shot me a look that told me to keep my mouth shut. I was happy to obey.

"I'm sure Loki's not the first young marine who's wanted to take a bite out of me." Colonel Levithan laughed. Lieutenant Schu laughed with him. I was just glad he understood. I figured that Loki couldn't be court-martialed for attacking a senior officer, but I sure could.

"As you were, gentlemen." The lieutenant guided the

colonel away, taking him on a tour of the base, talking about lines of fire and supply requests.

When they were out of hearing, Chang came up to me. "Dude," he said. "That was awesome. Loki is totally O.G."

I didn't answer him. I imagined the report in my file. I still couldn't control my dog.

Chang locked eyes with me, looking eager and earnest. "Can I, like, go again?"

"No way!" Vasquez was right beside him in a flash. "I changed my mind. I'm next. Let me wear the bite sleeve."

"Nah, bro, you didn't want to do it. You missed your shot," Chang said. "Anyone gonna bite you, it's Dempsey."

"My bark's worse than my bite," I said, and everyone stared at me in stunned silence.

"Well, look at that," Chang said. "Dempsey's got a sense of humor."

"Don't go thinking you won our bet," Douglass told him. "He didn't laugh."

"Oh, he will," Chang said. "Dempsey's got my back. We're like brothers! He wouldn't let me down."

"Just because he's your bro, don't make your jokes funny, Chang," Douglass replied. "You ain't *that* lucky."

We stood around trading insults and playing with Loki until the sun went down. Then I fed Loki and brushed his teeth and took him back to the small barracks to sleep. He looked at me like he did every night, asking to come up on the bed. I shook my head and pointed, and he sighed — he had a very loud, very clear sigh — and curled up on the floor by the side of the bed.

"Good job today, boy." I reached down to scratch his ears. "Very good boy."

In the middle of the night, the high-pitched screech of the monkeys woke me up.

Except they weren't monkeys this time.

"Incoming!" someone outside shouted, and a second later, a mortar screamed into the base, smashing into a sandbag with a roar and a deafening blast. Two more followed quickly after, parting gifts for the colonel, who'd flown out a few hours earlier. Our own machine guns roared to life, shooting their hot dragons' breath into the distant mountains.

"Screeeech!" Another shell whistled in and, when it hit just outside, shook dirt and dust loose from our ceiling.

"Tell the bad guys we're trying to sleep!" Chang groaned, pulling on his Kevlar helmet without even sitting up.

I reached over to check on Loki, to make sure he was okay with all the loud noises. My fingers hit nothing but cold floor.

I sat up and looked for him all around the bed.

He wasn't there.

"Loki!" I called. "Loki! Not now, buddy. Don't do this to me now . . ."

"What's going on?" Chang asked.

"It's Loki," I said. "He's gone AWOL."

"What?" Chang suddenly looked very awake.

"He's run off. I have to go find him."

"In the middle of a mortar attack?"

I didn't answer, just jammed my feet into my boots and ran outside with nothing else but my T-shirt, helmet, and boxers on. It was freezing, but I didn't care. Deadly mortars and grenades were falling onto the base, but I didn't care about that either.

"I'm coming with!" Chang grabbed his rifle and ran out after me, watching my back, just like on patrol. "You're crazy, bro!" he shouted over the rattle of machine-gun fire.

Maybe he was right. To run out into a mortar attack in my underwear, I must have been crazy. But I had to find Loki.

He was my partner.

SEMPER FIDO

I ran at a full sprint, calling Loki's name. Every few feet, marines were leaning on sandbags, their M16s smoking. They'd pop up over the bags and fire off a few rounds toward the mountains before ducking down again.

"Hold the small-arms fire!" Lieutenant Schumacher was hoarse from shouting. He'd clearly been sound asleep and was standing in his armor vest and helmet with sweatpants and sneakers. "There's no point in opening up with the M16s. You can't hit anything with them from here. Where's the 240?"

"Here!" Douglass came shuffling over, his massive machine gun cradled in his arms like a baby. Norris, a gangly kid from Colorado, was right behind him with belts of ammo.

"I want you to hit just above the tree line," Lieutenant Schumacher told him. "You hear me? It's the middle of the night and we're taking fire. Anyone moving on that hill is considered hostile, understood? Any movement you see is a target."

"Roger that." Douglass smiled. He set the gun down and started firing on full automatic. Hot brass casings ejected, steaming, from the weapon. Douglass had to shake them out of his boots as he fired. The spent ammo covered the ground like peanut shells after a circus. It jingled and crunched under my feet as I ran.

"Loki!" I called again.

The air screeched.

"Incoming!" someone shouted.

Chang tackled me against one of the heavy HESCOs and pressed me against it as the mortar round whistled in.

The mortar landed about fifteen feet above us on the hill, exploding in a shower of dirt and rock.

I was on my feet again before the dust had settled.

"Come on," Chang yelled at me. "Wait until this is over!"

"Get under cover," I yelled back at Chang. "Loki's my job. I'll find him myself!"

I couldn't believe Loki would pick now to go AWOL,

when things had been going so well. Maybe he was upset about the incident with the colonel. Maybe he was scared of the battle noise. Maybe, like on the first day I had him at training, he was just being difficult.

I ran around the outpost, ducking under fighting positions, dodging guys running back and forth with more ammo.

I didn't know where to look for Loki. He was a black dog, it was the middle of the night, and the noise and smoke of battle made the outpost's maze of HESCOs, sandbags, and razor wire even more confusing than usual.

I stopped running. Chang caught up to me as I caught my breath.

"Go back," I panted at him. "I got this."

Chang didn't answer me. I looked up at him, his eyes puffy with sleep, half dressed for combat and half for sleeping, but fully ready to assist, ready to follow me through hell to help me find my dog. And I had to admit, I needed help.

"I don't know where to look," I told him.

"We should check supply," Chang said. "I think I got an idea."

I nodded, and we were off again, scrambling down by the landing zone to the supply bunker.

We could see its door was open, but to get to it, we'd have to run across an open space. For a few seconds we'd be totally exposed to enemy fire from the mountain. It was dark, so maybe they wouldn't see us, but it was still a risk. If by chance a mortar hit nearby, there were no sandbags to stop hot metal shrapnel from tearing us apart.

"You can wait here," I told Chang. "He's my dog. My responsibility."

"He's a marine in my squad," said Chang. "He's *our* responsibility. And you asked for my help, so now you're getting it. *Semper Fi* means *always*, remember? Even for a dog. *Semper* Fido! Now what are you waiting for, Marine?"

He bolted into the open, sprinting for the other side. I ran after him, stumbling to keep up. About halfway across, the dirt kicked up around our feet with bullet impacts. The AK-47 — the enemy's machine gun of choice — wasn't very accurate, even at close range. They didn't have a chance at hitting us on purpose. But an accidental bullet in the chest was still a bullet in the chest.

I put my head down and charged like I was back on the high school football field, trying to break through an offensive line to sack the quarterback. I slammed right through the entrance to the supply bunker, knocking Chang to the floor with a grunt.

"You should play football," he groaned, pulling himself up and putting a hand out to me.

"I did," I said, grabbing his wrist and pulling myself off the floor. I scanned the area where we kept Loki's food and medical supplies.

Nothing there.

I looked at the box where we kept some of the training materials, the explosive samples and the timers and detonators. It was locked, and Loki wasn't around.

"Back here," said Chang. "I figured. He's here."

I ran to the back of the room and saw Loki tucked away in the shadows, looking up at me wide-eyed, his back quivering, afraid. He was curled up in a tight ball on top of a bundle of camouflage cloth. When I reached down for him, I saw that it was a patrol sleeping bag, the kind issued to every marine as part of his gear.

I tried to pull him off it, but he planted his legs, tucked in his tail, and pulled against me with all his strength. He didn't want to step off the bag.

"Hold on," said Chang. He bent down and peeked inside the bag. He nodded and showed me the name stenciled inside: Eliopulos, N. "Left here when they packed his things up. I thought that's what Loki might be after."

"You thought that?"

"I'm sentimental," said Chang. "Figured Loki might be too."

I let go of Loki's collar and he immediately curled back into a ball, burying his nose deep into the fabric of the bag.

Dogs have memories. That's how they can learn how to sit and stay and heel, how they can be trained to find bombs, and that's how they became man's best friend. They remember us by our smells. But memory can hurt too.

I remember the day my father left. I was on the couch playing a video game, something with soldiers fighting aliens. Mom and Dad were yelling at each other in their bedroom with the door wide open. She was holding Zach, who was just a baby. He didn't cry. He didn't make a sound.

"You don't understand a single thing!" my dad yelled.

"Oh I understand perfectly, Martin!" she yelled right back at him. "You think you're so tough. You've gotta fight everyone you see. That's not tough! That's weak. You're the weakest man I've ever met."

"Weak? You calling me weak?" He laughed in her face, a cruel, humorless laugh. "Let's see how you do without me, then. See if you can carry the weight of this family without me!"

He stormed out, slammed the front door. Didn't even pack a bag, just left.

"You think you're such a tough man!" she yelled after him, then yelled at the closed door where he had been. "Real men stay." She rested her forehead on it, her voice falling to a whisper. "Real men don't leave." She murmured to herself, but I could still hear her loud and clear. "Real men stay," she said again.

Dad didn't come back. Mom packed up his stuff, all of it, into a box and shoved it into the attic. She didn't throw anything away, but she erased every trace of him from the house. I remembered, though. I remembered him by the empty spaces, by the box in the attic, by the Marine Corps dress uniform wrapped in plastic inside it that he never came back to get.

Loki remembered his handler. He was just like me when Dad left. He couldn't understand what had happened to Corporal Eliopulos or why, but he knew that he'd had a handler that he trusted and slept beside and played with, and that that guy was gone. All that was left was this stinky old sleeping bag, abandoned in the back of the supply bunker.

I sat down next to Loki and ran my hand along his back.

"It's okay, pal," I told him. "I get it."

Chang watched us for a while without saying a word. When the outpost was quiet again, he peeked outside. "Looks like it's over for now," he said.

I urged Loki up and took the sleeping bag with us back to the barracks. The medical tent was empty, which meant we hadn't taken any casualties. Everyone who didn't have to be on watch was back in their racks trying to sleep. The middle-of-the-night attack was just the enemy's way of keeping us on our toes and keeping us tired. Some guys were already snoring. They weren't about to let the enemy claim a victory over their shut-eye.

I set the old sleeping bag down beside my bed and scratched Loki behind the ears.

"There you go, buddy," I told him. "You get some sleep now."

He curled up on the bag, burrowing into it as he let out a long, slow sigh. It might have meant nothing, just his way of exhaling after a stressful night. But I liked to think that it was his way of saying thank you.

I fell asleep with my hand hanging off the rack, resting on his head. He let my hand lie there all night, and he was still there when I woke up.

CHAPTER 15

FOOTFALL

That morning I got to check my e-mail on the satellite linkup.

Zach had written me.

> Hi Gus.
>
> I'm writing from school. Can you send a picture of you and Loki in your uniforms? No one believes me that my brother has a dog that outranks him. Do you feed him at the table too? Mom wants to know if you need anything sent in a care package? More bullets? Haha. School's good. I got an A in everything but math. Mom's good. She misses you. She told me not to ask you this, but did you kill any

dragons yet? I don't know what else to write. Come home soon. I'm tired of taking the trash out myself. And walking Baxter and TJ. They say hi too.

You know, in a dog way. — Zach

I stared at the screen for a while, picturing Zach on the other side of the world, taking care of Mom and the dogs and the house all by himself. Not that Mom needed taking care of. She was the toughest woman I'd ever met. She'd done so much for us on her own. I wanted to make her proud over here. I wanted to be tough for her. I knew she was scared that I'd get hurt or killed, or that war would break me like it broke my father. But I knew I took after her.

Like me, she didn't say much. She just wanted to know about what to send in a care package . . . I guess toughness comes in all different forms.

"Who's down with OPE?" I heard Chang rapping on the head down the hill. *"All the lay-dees!"*

I smirked and typed a quick reply to my brother:

Zebro — Will write more later. Heading out on a dragon hunt. Tell Mom to send Twinkies. — Gus.

As soon as we'd eaten breakfast, Lieutenant Schumacher called first platoon together for a briefing. Sergeant Gaffley and Staff Sergeant Luken stood next to him, writing notes in little green books they'd pulled from their pockets.

"We're going to check out some firing positions from last night's attack," the lieutenant told us. "They cannot fire on my outpost with impunity."

"Impunity?" Chang whispered to me. "He loves those SAT words."

"If it means building a patrol base on every damn ridge in this valley," Lieutenant Schu continued, "so help me, we will do it. The enemy won't be able to turn his head without running into Echo Company."

"Oo-rah!" we answered him in unison, before we rolled out of the base.

As usual, Chang, Loki, and I were walking point, out ahead of the platoon. We passed burned-out tree stumps and scorched patches of earth. We came to an abandoned compound with its door gaping open and its dirt walls crumbling. My squad was sent inside to search the courtyard.

Loki sniffed around every wall and under every rock, but all he came up with was an empty plastic water bottle and a chicken bone that he crunched on until I told him to drop it.

I was worried that the insurgents might leave things around that were tempting to dogs, to try to poison him.

We walked all morning without seeing any people. No shepherds or farmers or suspicious young men watching us warily in the distance. Nothing at all. It was creepy.

The fear of hidden IEDs was nothing like the fear of being in a firefight. With guns blazing all around and tracer fire streaking into the sky, a firefight is scary, but it's also exciting. Every move has a purpose, every moment comes into sharp focus. Time slows down and speeds up simultaneously, and it's kind of weird to admit it, but it's fun. The guns roar and spit fire, the noise shakes your bones, and you are fighting alongside your brothers. You don't have time to think about anything else, or worry about anything else. It's freeing.

But walking on a patrol, searching for explosives, knowing that you could set off a hidden bomb with every step . . . that just wears you out. It's all anticipation. It's all worry that your next footfall could be the one that kills you and everyone around you.

Everyone felt a little safer knowing that Loki's nose was on the job.

My eyes were fixed on him, about ten yards ahead, checking out another burned tree stump that looked like all the other burned tree stumps. But he kept pacing back and forth in front of it. I held my hand up in the air and the patrol stopped behind us.

Loki didn't sit down this time, but his behavior had changed enough that it was worth checking out. Chang and I stepped forward. I bent down to look at the ground and saw some wires sticking out.

"We've got something!" I called, whistling for Loki to come back with me to a safe distance so that Sergeant Gaffley could bring in the bomb disposal unit. He ran right beside me and nudged my pocket with his nose. I pulled out the toy and told him he was a good boy.

"I gotta teach Pixie to do something useful when I get back to Brooklyn," Chang said. "You think you could train a dog to get girls' phone numbers?" He raised his eyebrows, waiting for me to laugh. "Or to find Twinkies?"

I just shook my head, and Chang stepped over to my left, which is exactly what the bad guys thought he'd do.

They hadn't planted only one bomb.

They'd been watching me and Loki work for a few weeks now, and they'd figured us out. They planted one bomb for Loki to find, and they planted another one nearby, deeper, so the scent wouldn't be as strong.

That's the one Chang stepped on. We heard a click when his foot went down, and there was just enough time for eye contact. I saw Chang's face — a strange embarrassed look flashed across it, like he'd just run out of the house without pants on. It was too brief a moment to do anything.

The blast knocked me and Loki sideways. When I came to in a cloud of dirt, my ears ringing, Loki was already standing above me, panting anxiously.

I reached up, running my hands over him, checking his paws and his eyes, just like I'd learned in the first week of IDD training.

He was okay. I felt a moment of relief until my head cleared and I remembered Chang.

I heard shouts all around. The air was thick with smoke and my mouth was filled with a tangy, metallic taste.

Lieutenant Schumacher was on the radio calling for a medevac chopper.

"We've got one casualty and one KIA," he said.

It took my rattled brain a second to translate KIA into normal human talk. Killed in action. Dead. Someone was dead.

I pictured Chang's face again. That *oops* moment. He stepped in the wrong place.

Oops.

How long ago was it? A week? Ten seconds? Time had lost its meaning, events were unstitched. I heard my mother's voice in my head. "They'll chew you up and spit you out."

I felt sick to my stomach.

Vasquez rushed over, running his hands along my sides, shining a small flashlight into my eyes, checking me out like I'd just checked out Loki.

"Chang?" my voice creaked.

Vasquez shook his head. "You just chill out, all right? You took some shrapnel. You'll be fine, but we gotta get you on the chopper. Can you walk?"

I nodded and pushed myself off the ground. My legs hurt, but I could walk with Vasquez giving me support. Loki was at my side, staying right on my heel as we moved down the slope, past the other marines of first platoon who were pulling security for the incoming chopper. I looked behind me. Douglass and Norris were carrying Chang down behind us.

What was left of him, anyway.

I stopped and nearly tripped Vasquez as I bent down to throw up in the dirt.

"It's okay, Dempsey," he said. "Don't look, man. Just don't look."

Norris and Douglass kept moving past us, grimly determined to get Chang to the landing zone.

"I never laughed," I said.

Vasquez looked puzzled.

"I never laughed at one of Chang's jokes," I said. "He had a bet with Douglass that I would. I never did."

"Don't sweat it," Vasquez said. "Come on."

They piled me onto the chopper as it touched down. Loki jumped on with me. He started licking my face. It stung, but I didn't push him away. I held on to him.

The crew chief yelled something about Loki being onboard, but Staff Sergeant Luken came rushing over.

"The dog goes with his handler!" he shouted over the chopper's engines. Even if the crew chief couldn't hear him, he saw the staff sergeant insignia on his arm patches and the no-argument expression on his face and he nodded.

As we took off, Loki sniffed at the bag they'd loaded Chang's body into. It was right next to us. I squeezed Loki against me and held him tight, burying my face in his fur. That warm fur and dirty dog smell was the only thing that kept me from screaming.

CHAPTER 16

LEATHERNECK

I woke to the shriek of incoming fire. I scrambled from bed looking for my helmet and for Loki. It took me a second to realize where I was and that Loki wouldn't be on the floor next to me. There was no incoming fire. That was the sound of a plane landing.

I was recovering at Camp Leatherneck, the sprawling military base in southern Afghanistan. Just about every marine in-country passes through here at one time or another during their deployment. It's 1,600 acres of concrete barriers, portable housing units, headquarters and staff buildings, hot meals, hot showers, and a runway with supply planes screeching in and out, twenty-four hours a day, seven days a week.

"Jumpy much, Dempsey?" someone in another bed chuckled at me. "Why you so scared of an airplane?"

Fobbit, I thought. That's military elf talk actually taken right from one of the fantasy series I'd read to Zach.

Hobbits are fantastical little half-men in the Lord of the Rings books, lazy and comfortable, rarely leaving the comforts of their village.

Fobbits are military people who never leave the FOB — forward operating base. They take hot showers and eat hot food every day, and they don't understand why we infantry grunts are dirty and rude or why we flinch when we hear the shriek of an airplane. (It sounds just like an incoming rocket propelled grenade, that's why.)

I didn't know how long I'd been there. The doctors said I had a concussion. They wanted to check me out for a few days to make sure I hadn't suffered TBI — that stands for traumatic brain injury. The military elf talk got worse and worse the longer you spent in combat.

There was a box of Twinkies there for me, sent by my mother, so I'd either been unconscious for a while, or she'd used express shipping. Probably both.

I let the other guys recovering in the medical unit eat the bright yellow treats. They were never meant for me anyway. I'd wanted them for Chang.

The thing about Camp Leatherneck was that it wasn't

just a big military base for people. It was also for dogs. It held the dog kennels that supported all the K-9 teams within a thousand miles.

As soon as I was up and dressed, I left the fobbit in the next bed — I didn't even ask his name — and went to find the kennels to check on my dog.

Loki jumped and barked and panted as soon as he saw me step into the building. The air conditioning hummed steadily, keeping the dogs at a comfortable temperature.

"Hey," I said, squatting down in front of his cage. "How's my original gangsta?"

He shoved his face up against the wire and started licking me through it, his tail pounding against the ground. He didn't have his sleeping bag. I worried he'd miss it. I wondered what was happening up at the outpost. "How's my good boy?" I cooed at him.

"He's made some powerful friends," a voice behind me said. I turned around to see Diaz — Mama Bear — strolling in with his dog, Joker, by his side. He led Joker into the cage next to Loki's, put in a bowl of fresh water, and tossed him a treat. Joker scarfed it down and then went to sniff at Loki through the wire between their cages. "Colonel Levithan himself came to see Loki yesterday." He shook his head. "Told me they had 'history.' Whatever that means."

I shrugged. "How long you been in the 'Stan?"

"Just a week, man," he said. "I haven't even had to take a cold shower yet. It's like a beach resort here — minus the beach. I can't go home and tell my friends I spent the whole deployment on a base bigger than the town I grew up in. I wanna get outside the wire, get on a patrol."

"Appreciate the hot showers while you have them."

"I didn't sign up for the Corps to take hot showers. I mean — we learned to embrace the suck, right? It doesn't suck at all here."

"It'll suck soon enough," I told him. "Don't you worry about it. Pretty soon you'll smell like your dog." I smirked at him. "And it'll be an improvement."

He smiled back at me. "Loki must be getting to you," he said. "You're actually being friendly."

I looked down at Loki in his cage. He was rolling around on his back, throwing his legs from side to side, and then popping up on all fours again, over and over, just for the fun of it.

"Can't spend so much time with a dog and not be a little more human, I guess."

"Dude," Diaz gaped at me. "When did you turn into a warrior poet?"

"Same time you turned into a dimwit," I smirked at him again.

"No," Diaz laughed. "I was born this way. You hear about Hulk?"

"No," I said, my voice catching in my throat. I didn't like his tone of voice. There was no laughter in it.

He shook his head. "First day here, flying out from Leatherneck to some patrol base farther south, had mechanical problems and the chopper crashed. No one was killed, but he shattered his foot, broke his wrist, and lost an eye. Discharged. His dog too — wouldn't go near a helicopter after that. I think Hulk's gonna adopt him. Shortest deployment I ever heard of."

I nodded. I pictured Chang again, just before he stepped on the bomb. I shuddered.

"Could have been worse," I told Diaz.

He didn't push me to explain. He knew.

"Corporal Gus Dempsey?" A private stepped into the kennel, a piece of paper clutched in his hand.

"That's me."

"Colonel Levithan wants to see you."

166

"Now?"

The young marine rolled his eyes at me. "No, next week. The colonel loves waiting around for enlisted grunts."

"Chill, bro," Diaz told the guy. "Dempsey's got brain damage."

"I'm, uh, sorry, I . . ." the marine stumbled, not sure what to say.

"Don't sweat it," Diaz laughed. "It's actually made him a lot more likable."

I laughed. It wasn't all that funny, but it felt good to laugh. And the look on the private's face was priceless.

"I don't have time for this," he said. "I've been looking for Dempsey all day."

"All day?" I said. "I've only been out of bed for half an hour."

"What's the colonel want with Dempsey, anyway?" Diaz asked, suddenly protective of me. I guess we had "history" too.

"Do I look like someone Colonel Levithan confides in?" The guy was annoyed now. "Let's go."

I turned back to my dog. "Don't worry, Loki. We'll get you back home soon."

"Home?" It was Diaz's turn to raise his eyebrows at me.

"Nothing says home like a cold rack and pit latrines," I laughed, but I was really surprised myself. Why had I called that dusty, dirty, dangerous outpost home?

"I guess there's no place like it," Diaz shook his head. Then he looked me up and down with a smile. "Dempsey-Wempsey, summoned by the colonel." He gave me a fist bump. I returned it, but the sideways smirk on his face made me think of Chang.

"Later, Mama Bear," I called back, and followed the private outside.

Loki didn't take his eyes off me as I left. I heard a whine from his cage.

"I'll be right back," I told him, and I hoped he understood. And I hoped it was true. We'd failed to protect Chang, failed to detect the other bomb. Maybe this was it. Maybe I was going to be sent home, a failure.

I hopped into the private's jeep for a quick ride over to the headquarters, suddenly worried this would be the end of me and Loki as a team. If they sent me packing, would they even give me time to say good-bye to my dog? The Marine Corps wasn't a sentimental bunch.

Colonel Levithan stood when I entered the room. "Corporal." He offered me a seat.

"Sir." I saluted and sat down. I was grateful. I felt a little woozy on my feet.

"I read your lieutenant's report on the incident," he said. "You and your dog are doing fine work. It could have been a lot worse without you there."

It couldn't have been worse for Chang, I thought, but I kept my mouth shut. I guess I wasn't getting in trouble after all.

"The Corps takes brain injuries very seriously, son," he said. "So I'll put this to you pretty plain. We've got a battalion-wide op coming up in your company's battle space."

I had to translate in my head from military elf into human speak. He meant an entire battalion — about a thousand marines — were going to conduct some sort of operation around the area of Outpost Eliopulos.

"We're going to flush them out of the valley and cut off their escape routes across the border. It works kind of like hunting with dogs, driving birds from the bush. In this case, the dogs are a few rifle companies and they are going into the villages in the valley to route out enemy fighters. When those fighters come running to escape through the mountains, another rifle company — Echo Company — will be waiting to engage them."

I couldn't figure out why he was telling me all this. He

was so far above my rank he might as well have been the president. Why did I need to know this stuff?

"You want to get back to your company, Corporal?"

"Yes, sir," I said.

"Given your injuries, we cannot order you back. Not in time to participate in this op," he said.

"Yes, sir," I said.

"But if you request to return . . ." His voice trailed off. "Those mountain passes are filled with places to hide IEDs. Our guys would be a lot safer with an experienced dog team on the ground. I want you to think about it for a day or two, Corporal."

"Yes, sir."

"I can't order you," he repeated.

"I understand, sir."

"That is all," he said.

I stood and saluted. He dismissed me, and I made my way back to the kennel.

I wanted to take Loki for a walk. I had some serious thinking to do, and I guess I wanted to do it with my partner at my side. If I volunteered to go back and take part in this operation, it wouldn't just be my life I was putting in danger. It would be Loki's life too.

CHAPTER 17

FETCH

Back home, before the Corps, whenever I had a problem I needed to work out or something was bothering me, I'd take Baxter and TJ for a walk.

It's a simple thing, walking a dog. It wasn't like taking them outside to go to the bathroom, and it definitely wasn't like going hunting. There was no point to it but the walk. The walk *was* the point. As my dogs trotted around me, sniffing at whatever caught their interest, I could relax a little, not worry about what anyone thought of me, or how I was doing on the football team or in school. Or if I was living up to the idea of myself I had in my head. I could just be a guy walking his dogs. And I found it easier to talk to them than to talk to most people.

Loki trotted beside me now as we made our way through

the desert dust of Leatherneck. He peed on the side of a metal storage unit that had been turned into an officer's quarters. I hoped no one was watching him.

He stuck close to me. It was our first walk since the patrol. I knew it had been a week because that's what they told me, but I'd fallen out of time. Camp Leatherneck felt like a dream. Airplanes shaking the walls as they took off and landed day and night, air conditioning and showers, a gym and a hospital. There was even a makeshift plywood pool hall. Laughter shook its walls day and night.

"So what do you think, O.G. Loki?" I asked.

Chang's face popped into my head again, his sideways smile tilting into the sun like a ramp. I figured this was how it would be now. Chang would go on my walks too. There were worse ghosts to be haunted by than your friends, I guessed.

Loki stopped and curled around to lick his back leg.

"Here's the situation," I told him. He looked up at me. He knew I was talking to him. Even if he couldn't understand the words, he knew they were meant for him. "They need us at OPE, you know that? We have a big job to do. Dangerous."

Loki cocked his head, as if to say, *Is that it?*

I guess that wasn't it.

"We don't have to go back yet," I said. "It's up to us."

It wasn't all about the marines. Mom and Zach needed me too. Zach was worried — or else he wouldn't have bothered writing from school. And Zach would only worry if he saw Mom worrying. The Twinkies were just her way of showing it.

But her worries weren't only that I'd get hurt. She was worried I'd become a different person, someone moody and angry and distant, like my father had. She was worried that even if I came back, I would leave a part of myself over here. Should I be volunteering for danger, knowing how she felt?

And if I didn't, what kind of person would I become then? What kind of man would I come back as, knowing I'd let down my friends?

The guys up at OPE did need us, but after all that had happened, I needed them too. Everything at the outpost was important. Everything we said or did, we did with the knowledge that it could be life or death. Everything mattered. How could I go back to taking out the trash at home, when I'd walked point on a patrol and searched strangers' homes for explosives? When I'd sat next to my friend on the head, listening to him rap, looking across the valley at the mountains, and hoping that an attack didn't come in before I got off the toilet?

I couldn't. Not without knowing I'd given it my all. It wasn't anything like home, but it wasn't like anywhere else either.

Kind of like Loki's sleeping bag. The place was filled with familiar smells, gross as they were.

"What do you think we should do, Loki?" I asked him. "We can stay safe down here for a while. Miss the big, dangerous op. Another team will go. You think that's what Mom would want us to do?"

Loki looked up at me when I talked to him, and figuring that meant playtime, I guess, he whacked me with his paw, right in the pocket.

"Okay, okay," I told him. I pulled out the toy. He sat and licked his lips. I moved it from side to side, watching his eyes track it. Then I tossed the toy as hard as I could in a great, soaring arc. Loki raced after it, a black streak across the desert.

In a flash, he was back. He dropped the toy at my feet and looked up at me, doing a little dance with his front paws, ready to give chase again. I picked up the toy and threw. He charged, leaping over ruts in the dirt, front and back legs working in unison, zigzagging across the sand. He looked like he was flying.

Watching him run, I felt a pang of doubt.

He didn't sign up for this. As much I liked to think that he knew he was a marine with important work to do, he didn't really know the difference between this game of fetch and the work we did on patrol. He was born to train as an IDD dog, and with each test he passed and each round of training, he was bustled forward into a life he hadn't chosen. And now, he was with me because he'd been assigned to me, just like he'd been assigned his last handler.

But was my life so different? I'd been trained, I'd been assigned to Outpost Eliopulos. The only reason Chang and I knew each other was an accident of fate. I just as easily could have known some other guys at some other base or gotten sent home after a crash like Hulk. I just as easily could have stepped on that bomb instead of Chang. It was all random.

But it still mattered. The people around us, even if we didn't choose them, mattered. The things that happened, even if they happened without any rhyme or reason we could see, mattered. We couldn't choose everything that would happen to us, but we could choose how we handled it as it happened.

175

Loki brought the toy back. I picked it up to throw again.

"You want this? You want it?" He barked and spun. He jumped to grab it from my hand, and I had to yank it away at the last second. He hit the ground, and I threw it in the opposite direction.

"Go! Go!" I yelled, and he was off again. Nothing else mattered to him at that moment but getting that toy and bringing it back.

I remembered what Chang said to me that first night, quoting the Batman movie. It was the same thing Loki said with every bark and every wag of his tail: Why so serious?

Loki didn't know we were in a war or doing important work. He just knew he felt a bond with his marines, and especially with me. That was all he needed. He didn't know what came next, and it didn't matter. The connection was all that mattered. That was why he whined when I left him alone, why he felt safe in his old handler's sleeping bag, why he wanted to play as much as possible.

He hadn't chosen me or chosen this job, but he was doing it with joy, doing his best and wagging his tail through it all. He was afraid when there were things to be afraid of, and he was playful when there were things to play with, and he was a goof when I needed a goof, even if I didn't know that's what I needed. He just loved the humans around him while he could, as much as he could, and brought his best every day.

Toughness wasn't about being the strongest or the biggest or the baddest, it was about seeing the job through, even when it was hard, sticking by your friends. My mother would understand why I chose to stay. Loyalty was toughness. *Semper Fi*. Always faithful. Loki didn't need that explained to him. He lived that way.

So would I.

Real men stay.

Loki and I played fetch all afternoon, until the sun set and Loki began to vanish into the shadows each time I threw the toy. He always came back out of the darkness to drop the toy at my feet and beg me to throw it again.

Once it was dark, I went over to one of the big bunkers the military set up for us to get online. A few marines sat at other terminals, writing e-mails or checking Facebook or video chatting with their families back in America. Loki lay down on the dirty floor at my feet and gnawed on his toy.

I logged in to my e-mail and found the picture I was looking for. Douglass had sent it sometime during the week I'd been unconscious.

The picture showed me standing in the hazy background during our demonstration for the colonel. In sharp focus at the center of the picture, Loki was wrestling Chang down to the ground, his black fur bristling, red dust rising in the air around his feet. Chang had his arm raised with Loki pulling on the end of it, his teeth buried deep in the bite sleeve. Chang's white teeth shone with laughter, frozen forever in that picture's pose.

I smiled looking at it, then typed a new message.

Hey, Zebro. Here's that pic you wanted. That's me in the background, and in front, that's two of the toughest marines in the world. They're both heroes. I'm still learning to be. *Semper Fi,* bro. — Gus

I hit send and stood up.

"Well, Loki," I said, picking up his toy and leading him out into the cool desert night at Camp Leatherneck. Generators rumbled loudly as we walked back toward the kennels. "You ready to go back into the mountains?"

His tail wagged, and I knew he understood. He was going back to his friends, wherever they needed him to be.

And so was I.

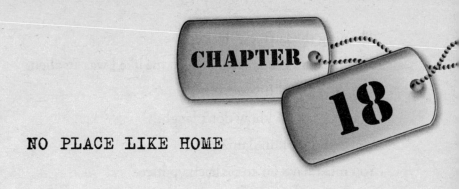

CHAPTER 18

NO PLACE LIKE HOME

"Something don't smell right." Douglass stood in the doorway to the narrow bunker, sniffing the air. "Is that . . . shampoo that I smell? Did some marine just get back from a spa?"

"Good to see you too, Douglass," I said, standing up to greet him.

"Bad guys gonna smell you from across the valley and know just where to aim. You the only clean thing in a hundred miles."

I was definitely the cleanest guy on base. Even Loki was cleaner than any of the marines up on the outpost.

"Now that you're back, we gotta get you an OPE shower," he added.

"What's that?"

"Cleaning the latrines," he said.

I laughed, and Douglass looked at me like I was an alien.

"What?" I said. "It was funny."

"The Dempsey I know don't laugh."

"Maybe I got brain damage."

"You must have, to come back up here."

"Loki insisted. I think he had a date with Vasquez."

"I knew the two of them had something special."

We joked like that for a few more minutes. The jokes kept us going without having to talk about Chang, at least not directly. But we were also kind of talking about him the whole time. If his death had made us stop messing with each other, he would have taken it as a great insult to his memory.

I went out to take a walk around the base. It was pitch-black outside, but Loki could lead me. I liked the late nights up at OPE. Lieutenant Schu and Staff Sergeant Luken were asleep. Vasquez was up, sorting bandages. He welcomed us back by tackling Loki and wrestling with him in the dirt. So much for a clean dog.

"Will you shut up?" someone grunted from inside the barracks. "Some of us are trying to sleep through the war!"

Vasquez dusted himself off and stood up. "Welcome back, brother," he said to me. "Word is you volunteered to come back sooner than you had to. What was the problem? You didn't like the heated towels at Leatherneck?"

I laughed.

"Seriously, though, Dempsey," he said. "We're glad to have you and your O.G. back here. Everybody feels a lot better with Loki looking out for us."

I glanced over at the medical supplies he had laid out, bandages and needles, packets of fluids and pain killer pills. Like he was expecting a lot of casualties.

"Lieutenant Schu's briefing us in the morning about Hunting Dog," he said.

"Hunting Dog?"

"That's the name of the operation," Vasquez answered. "I think the colonel took a liking to Loki, named it in his honor."

Loki, hearing his name, rolled onto his back, demanding Vasquez rub his belly. Vasquez obeyed, and Loki's tongue rolled happily out of his mouth.

Then we heard the screech of an incoming attack. The quiet of the nighttime was torn open. Men shouted as they scrambled from their bunks and rushed to fighting positions. I grabbed Loki and pulled him close as Vasquez and I jumped into a sandbag bunker. Loki panted happily in my arms. Even with the deafening explosions of the bombs and the roar of the machine guns, his tail wagged.

The attack was over almost as soon as it had started. We climbed out of the bunker. Douglass was taking apart his gun, even though it was still smoking hot.

"Gun jammed," he said. Hot brass shell casings littered the ground at his feet.

"Or you melted the barrel," Vasquez suggested.

"Doesn't matter much," Douglass shrugged. "They didn't have much fight in them tonight. Probably just saw the helicopter come in and wanted to welcome our dog team back to us. Give you a proper fireworks display."

I picked up a piece of hot, twisted metal from the dirt, a vicious bit of shrapnel that easily could have killed one of us.

"Some welcome," I grunted.

Loki sniffed at the metal in my hand and wagged his tail. To him, it must have smelled just like everything else I asked him to find. He jumped up and leaned on me with his front paws to get a really good sniff at it. Then he nudged my pocket with his snout.

Time to play, Boss, he seemed to say. *That smell means it's time to play.*

I pulled out his toy and let him tug on it for a while.

"O.G. Loki," Vasquez laughed. "He comes out of a fire-fight and wants to play. Now, that's a marine."

He barked, which I guess was his way of saying *oo-rah*.

"Glad you guys are back." Douglass patted me on the shoulder and gave me a long look. Finally, he smirked. "Because I wasn't kidding about that OPE shower. Those latrines are nasty. You best get them cleaned up and get yourself dirty by morning. We've got some hunting to do."

COLLATERAL DAMAGE

We loaded onto two big helicopters under the cover of darkness, geared up and ready for battle. Loki even had on his dog body armor. He didn't act goofy or roll over for belly rubs or nuzzle my pocket for the toy. It seemed like he knew something important was happening.

Apache gunships armed with hellfire missiles and explosive-tipped bullets buzzed back and forth over our heads, ready to escort us to our landing zone.

Lieutenant Schu had briefed us first thing in the morning.

"Echo Company will be spread along this ridge." He showed us a big map, drawing a line across the mountains with his fingers. "As Alpha Company flushes the enemy out of the village in the valley, they are going to head for the border behind us. We're going to stop them from getting across. Dog team!"

"Yes, sir," I said.

"First off, glad to have you guys back. We've missed our Loki all week."

"Glad to be back, Lieutenant," I said. Loki wagged his tail.

"There's a compound *here*." He jabbed his finger at the map, pointing at a spot near the ridge line. "Intel suggests that a bomb-maker might be operating a safe house out of that place. I'm going to want you and first platoon to clear that compound as soon as we land. If they run — and they will run, they always run — second and third platoon will be here and here" — He showed us on the map — "to mop them up. Then we'll wait quietly inside to see who comes knocking."

"Yes, sir," I said.

And just like that, Loki and I had our orders. I wondered if the bomb-maker we were after had planted the IED that killed Chang. Part of me hoped so. I'd love to be the guy that caught him.

On board the helicopter, I leaned my head against the metal frame and closed my eyes, imagining Loki and me standing in the bomb-maker's compound. It looked like a medieval fortress in my imagination, something from one of my brother's books. There were orcs and ghouls and trolls swarming around us and Loki and I fought bravely through them, sword and tooth, to the dragon's lair. Instead of gold, this dragon guarded bombs and it opened its mouth to blow us away. But my sword pierced its throat, and the dragon fell. The orcs and ghouls and trolls stopped fighting and cheered. They had been enslaved to the dragon, and now they were free. Loki and I had saved them.

I snapped my eyes open. It's crazy where your mind goes when you're tired. I looked over at Douglass and saw graffiti scrawled along the metal hull just beside him. *Never trust an aircraft under thirty*, it read. I smiled. This was the same helicopter that had brought me to the outpost on my first night.

I felt us suddenly losing altitude at a sharp angle. My stomach lurched into my throat. It was like the big drop on a roller coaster. Everyone started checking their weapons and securing their rucksacks, getting ready to dismount the second we landed. I scratched Loki behind the ears.

"You ready, pal?" I whispered.

The wheels hit the ground and the doors opened. Marines jumped out and scrambled away from the chopper, kneeling and lying down, their guns pointing out to secure the landing zone. Loki and I leaped down, and I raised my gun up, just like I'd been trained. Loki, still on his leash attached to my belt, stood alert at my side, his ears perked, one front leg lifted slightly off the ground. Hunting position. He was ready. The chopper vanished into the darkness.

My team moved out, over the top of the ridge and down toward the compound. We stayed off the trail, which we were sure would be rigged with hidden explosives, and picked our way slowly along the rocky terrain.

The compound was carved into the mountainside, about three hundred yards below us. A dry riverbed snaked along the valley floor beneath it, and high mountains rose on the other side, dwarfing the compound, which was really just a small cluster of buildings with baked mud walls. It didn't look anything like a medieval fortress. It was a peasant's compound with a flimsy wooden gate locked with a rusty padlock, not a dragon's lair. But in this war, the dragons looked like everyone else.

I took up the point position, with Douglass by my side, guarding. I let Loki off his leash to sniff our way down, in case there were explosives hidden along the approach. He walked about twenty yards ahead and I kept my eyes fixed, watching him for any change of behavior, any clue that we were in trouble. I felt a lump in my throat, worried that his armor wasn't thick enough, worried that it was too heavy and he'd set off a pressure activated bomb that he could have just walked over fine without the armor on. Every action and its opposite put Loki in danger. I wanted to call him back by my side, to keep him safe.

But that wasn't his job. I needed to clear my head, stop thinking about secret dragons and hidden dangers, and just let him work. I had to trust my partner.

We reached the compound wall and assembled in front of it. Douglass pulled out a sawed-off shotgun. He muttered a small prayer to himself, then pointed the gun at the lock on the gate. A smirk spread across his face. He looked over at me.

"For Chang," he said. I nodded, and he pulled the trigger.

The lock on the gate disintegrated with the blast. Douglass kicked the door open, and threw a flashbang, which is a grenade that doesn't kill anyone, just makes a huge noise and a bright flash of light. It confuses and disorients people. I imagined that waking up to a platoon of marines bursting into your house would already be confusing and disorienting enough, but we didn't take any chances. The marines streamed inside.

I moved in at the back of the line to start the sweep, but as soon as we'd all crossed into the compound, the shooting erupted. I tackled Loki back out the door again as bullets tore up the mud wall around us.

"Shooter upstairs!" Douglass shouted, and the entire platoon unleashed a hail of bullets into an upper room.

"Contact," Sergeant Gaffley said into his radio, describing our situation to the lieutenant back on the ridge and to headquarters at Camp Leatherneck. He had to shout over the crack of gunfire. A cloud of smoke and dust swirled around us.

"Hold your fire!" the sergeant yelled. The order echoed down the line as marines passed it along. The compound grew quiet. Somewhere in the distance, a stray dog barked. The air smelled heavy with metal and smoke and left an acid taste on my tongue. I could only imagine how unpleasant it smelled to Loki.

After a moment, through the heavy quiet, we heard a wailing. A woman's voice, crying out, screaming. Vasquez started up the rickety wooden stairs to check it out, but Sergeant Gaffley stopped him.

"Dempsey!" he called. "You and Loki check that out. Could be a booby trap. Douglass, cover them."

Douglass snapped back the bolt on his big M240. The sound alone was probably enough to give any bad guys second thoughts about lifting their heads.

I leaned down and pressed my face into the fur between Loki's ears. "Here we go, pal," I whispered. "Time to protect our friends." I ruffled his fur, unclipped his leash, and sent him up the stairs ahead of us. He sniffed around eagerly, scanning for any smells that would mean a reward. He sniffed at every step and every crack in the wall. I held my position, keeping my eyes fixed on his back, terrified that the dark doorway above would light up with gunfire.

He approached the doorway, sniffed around the edge, and then looked back at me, his face a question mark.

Vasquez tensed beside me. "Does that mean he found something?"

"No," I told him. "He's just wondering if he can look inside." I gave Loki the hand signal to go in. He vanished into the doorway, and I held my breath. Seconds later, the woman started screaming again, and Loki was barking.

I ran up the stairs, taking them two at a time. My foot crashed through a rotten one and I almost fell over the side, but I caught the railing, and I made it to the top. I didn't hesitate to rush through the doorway. I didn't even consider that the enemy could be waiting on the other side, ready to shoot the first marine who came through. My partner needed me.

"Loki, heel!" I shouted as I entered the room.

There was no enemy fighter, but we weren't alone in the room.

A woman in a full veil that covered her from head to foot was sitting on the floor, swatting at Loki with a stick to keep him away. He growled and barked at her threats but kept his distance. In her other arm, cradled across her lap, she held the limp body of a girl whose clothes were stained with red. I saw the stains blossoming in front of me. Blood. The woman wailed again, a cry like I'd never heard before.

Vasquez came into the room behind me. The moment he saw the woman and the little girl, he lowered his weapon and rushed to her.

"Let me help you," he said, his voice as soothing as he could make it.

He knelt down in front of the woman and started checking the girl for signs of life. He looked back at me and shook his head. As he did, I noticed around his knees that there were spent shell casings.

Someone had been firing on us from this room. A room with a child in it.

In military elf, damage to property and injury to innocent persons in the course of battle is called *collateral damage*. Every side of a war makes decisions about what kinds of collateral damage they can live with — or what they're willing to risk in order to win. Whoever had been shooting at us from this room had made a decision with major consequences for this woman and this girl, and we were looking at the results.

Or maybe the woman and child had chosen to be here for the same reasons I had. You stick by the people you love, even when it's dangerous.

I bit down on the inside of my cheek to keep my focus on the job, and commanded Loki to search, doing my best to ignore the woman's cries as Vasquez tried to calm her. Marines streamed into the room.

"We've got civilian casualties," the sergeant called into the radio. The woman was yelling now, but the translator was with one of the other platoons. We had no idea what she was saying. I could imagine some things I'd be saying if I were her.

I chased those thoughts from my mind and focused again on Loki. He sniffed at the walls and the bed and the floorboards. He stopped at a rug and sniffed some more. He paced over it. He stopped and sat down.

"We've got something!" I yelled. The room tensed. The woman's head snapped to the side to look right at my dog through her veil, and then she really started yelling. She threw her stick at him, and it hit Loki right in the side. With his armor on, he hardly noticed; he thought she was playing. His tail wagged.

I knew she wasn't playing, and so did the rest of my platoon.

"Hey!" Vasquez yelled at her and stood, pointing his gun in her face. All his kindness wiped away. "Calm down, now!" he yelled.

"She could have a trigger!" someone else yelled.

Everybody froze. Who knew if she was wearing a bomb under her veil? It wasn't unheard of for terrorists to strap explosives to women and children, to turn their bodies into weapons. We were up against an enemy that had used a room with a woman and a child in it for cover, knowing we would fire back. Who knew what else they would do? We all waited, holding our breath, our fingers on our triggers.

Zach popped into my head. After all this war, I still hadn't seen a dragon to fight. Just kitchen timers, exploding mounds of dirt, and frightened, angry people.

"It's okay," I told Vasquez. "Loki didn't smell anything on her. He smelled right here!"

Vasquez lowered his gun. The woman went back to shouting. Douglass came over and together we inspected the carpet for trip wires. Once we saw it was clear, we rolled it back. There was a trapdoor beneath it. I raised my gun into firing position, and Douglass raised his. Sergeant Gaffley lifted the wood up, and we saw a drop-off beneath the floor, with daylight streaming through.

"Must lead outside," Douglass said.

I was about to say I agreed with him when Loki barked once and bolted past me, diving into the trapdoor and running toward the daylight.

"Loki, come!" I yelled after him, but he ignored me. He'd caught a scent and he was after it. I cursed under my breath at his stubbornness and jumped in after my partner.

"Dempsey!" Sergeant Gaffley shouted. "Get your butt back here!"

But by then, I was already gone.

CHAPTER 20

STRAYS

I squeezed through a narrow hole in the rear wall and popped up outside the compound. Loki was running full speed down the slope of the hill toward the dry riverbed, and I ran after him.

I saw two AK-47s, the terrorists' favorite machine gun, lying in the dirt. The men who'd fired on us in the compound must have ditched their weapons when they'd fled so that they could try to blend in with the civilian population. If we hadn't found their trapdoor, they would have come back for their guns after we'd gone.

I noticed a blood trail on the rocks. Loki seemed to be chasing it. He was already a hundred yards ahead of me, moving like lightning even in his heavy body armor. I sprinted to keep up.

I looked past him and saw two figures running ahead. I could tell one was injured, but they were both moving fast up the far slope of the hill toward the caves, where they probably thought they could hide.

Or maybe they had reinforcements waiting. I couldn't think too hard about it. I ran so fast, so focused on my dog, that I didn't notice at first that Douglass and Vasquez and the others had stayed behind.

Of course they had. The sun had risen above the mountains, so I was totally visible in the valley. If a team from the compound had followed me, it would be a sure way to reveal our position to the enemy and ruin Operation Hunting Dog before it had even started.

I was on my own. But I wasn't completely alone.

A pack of three stray dogs had picked up our scent and were approaching from the side of the dry riverbed, their eyes fixed on Loki. He noticed them too and stopped running to turn in their direction, the hair on his back rising. The enemy fighters moved farther up the opposite slope.

The stray dogs kept coming toward Loki. I needed to get to him first. I kicked at the dirt and skittered down the hill. I bolted across the dry riverbed, leaping over rocks and piles of garbage, tangled plastic bags, and mounds of dirt.

Loki was in trouble. The three mangy dogs, wiry and scarred, tried to flank him, their hackles up, their heads lowered. I knew the behavior from hours spent hunting with Baxter and TJ back at home. They were about to pounce. Loki mirrored them. He was a marine — he was not about to back down.

I was sure that Loki could handle himself in a dogfight, but he was outnumbered and these dogs might carry all kinds of diseases. At the same time, the bad guys were getting away. I had to intervene. When I reached Loki, I charged in front of him, putting my body between him and the strays, and I leveled my rifle at them.

"Back off," I commanded, hoping that the tone of my voice would scare them into submission.

It didn't.

They kept pacing before us. I kept my gun at the ready.

As much as I hated the idea of killing dogs, if they attacked, I would shoot them. I had no choice. My finger rested on the trigger and I started backing away, urging Loki to back up behind me.

The first dog barked. I glanced up the hill toward the guys running away. One of them looked back at me. I was glad they'd dropped their rifles because right now they had a clear shot at me and at Loki, both. And we were totally distracted. If there were any other guys in the hills who hadn't dropped their weapons, we'd be easy targets.

"We can't stay here, Loki," I whispered to him. "I'm sorry."

It seemed unfair, what I was about to do, and I really wished Loki didn't have to see it. I took aim at the first dog, hoping I got a clean shot, hoping he wouldn't suffer. I wondered if the first shot would scare off the other two or if I would have to put them all down. Thoughts of Baxter and TJ at home ran through my head. I took another step back. Loki barked. The three strays barked back, and just then, a loud explosion jolted us all.

My head snapped in the direction of the explosion, up on the hills. I saw one of the bad guys scrambling away from a cloud of smoke and dust. The other one lay a few feet below him, totally still. They had stepped on one of their own bombs, I figured. The strays ran off, back in the direction they'd come, frightened by the blast. I kept my gun pointed their way as they ran, in case they got the idea to turn back. Relief trickled down my back like a hot shower. I hadn't come here to hurt dogs. I'd gotten very lucky.

I turned to Loki and glanced back across the valley to the compound we'd raided. I looked in the other direction toward the hill where the terrorist was fleeing. If I turned back with Loki now, we'd be safer, but the terrorist would get away and he'd keep trying to kill us. If I caught him, he could help us find where he'd hidden explosives. He could help us learn how he got his supplies. He could lead us to other terrorists. If I caught him, I could find out if he'd planted the bomb that killed Chang.

Loki looked up at me, his big brown eyes wide, his face eager for instruction. He would follow me anywhere. The choice was mine.

I tapped my pocket where his toy was tucked. His tail wagged. I pointed up toward the hill, toward the man running from us. "Get him, go!" I commanded, and Loki was off like a bullet.

I ran after him, holding my gun at the ready.

CHAPTER 21

THE DRAGON

At the top of a ridge, Loki paced back and forth, sniffing around the mouth of a small cavern. I came up to him, panting, winded from my run up the hill. When he saw me, he stood perfectly still, his nose pointed at the dark hole in the rocks.

"Good boy," I whispered, crouching beside the opening to the cave. I really didn't want to go charging into the dark. I pulled Loki beside me and I called down into the gaping black maw of the rock, my M16 raised into firing position just in case.

"Come out!" I ordered. "Come out with your hands above your head!"

No response came. I didn't really think it would. The

man inside probably didn't even understand me. I looked down at Loki and held my finger in front of his face.

"Stay," I commanded. "Stay."

I stood and spun, moving into the darkness. The light behind me stretched my shadow deep inside the cave, making my silhouette too easy a target. I moved closer to the wall, pressing myself into the shadows, the barrel of my gun pointed forward, my finger on the trigger.

The cave wasn't deep. It was more like an alcove in the rocks. There were old ashes in a burned-out fire pit, but no other evidence that told me when the cave was last used. It could have been the night before; it could have been years.

The terrorist was leaning against the rear wall, half in shadow, half in light. I saw his dirty gray robe and ripped pants, stained with blood. One hand clutched a wound on his leg. I moved my gun barrel up his body, my eyes moving with it, and I saw his face. His lips moved as he murmured softly to himself.

He was young, my age or maybe a little younger. He had just the first wisps of a beard. His hair was matted and tangled, his lips cracked and chapped. And he was praying. I didn't know what he was saying, but I'd heard the words enough in movies and on TV. Something about Allah, which was the Arabic word for God. His free hand was shaking. He was terrified.

"Come on," I ordered him. "Hands up. I'm not going to hurt you."

He kept praying.

"Hands! Up!" I yelled and tried to demonstrate with one hand, still gripping my gun in the other.

He looked up at me, eyes going wide, and prayed faster, louder.

That's when I saw the detonator switch in his hand. A wire ran from it into his sleeve. I could make out the bulge under his robe where he was obviously wearing a belt filled with explosives. We'd been trained to identify the signs of hidden bombs strapped to a person, called a "suicide belt" or "suicide vest."

I never thought I'd be face-to-face with one.

His fist was clenched tight on a dead man's switch. It was designed so that if he let go, the bomb would go off. That way, if I shot him, his hand would open and he would explode, taking me with him.

I thought about Mom at that moment, and about Zach and his elves and dragons. At least now I knew. This is what the dragon looked like: a scared guy in a cave, a guy my age who probably thought about girls and laughed at dirty jokes and wanted to be a hero in someone's eyes. I guess this is what he thought he had to do to be a man. Maybe he had a little brother. Maybe his little brother was the kid with the goats who Chang gave the stick of gum.

"You don't have to do this," I whispered.

He kept praying.

Then Loki charged into the cave, rushing past me.

"No!" I shouted. "Out! Out!" But Loki was stubborn, and he smelled the smell he'd been trained to find, the smell of explosives. Or maybe he just sensed I was in danger, maybe he could smell my fear. He had no way of knowing what would come next.

The guy's eyes went wide. He shouted something, and I saw his hand open as I stumbled backward, reaching for Loki, hoping to pull him away before it was too late, before the flash and the blast and the end.

The last sound I heard was Loki's gleeful bark, telling me he'd found something, hoping it was now time to play.

CHAPTER 22

SEEK

I came to with my ears ringing, gasping for air, desperate for air. I inhaled a sharp breath that tasted of metal. I was dizzy and my face stung. My leg hurt. The pain told me I was still alive.

"Loki," I croaked out, unsure if my voice made any sound at all. It felt as if a great weight was pressing on me. I pushed with all the strength I had and rolled out from underneath a heap of jagged rock. The earth around me smoked. There was little left of the cave or of the bomber.

As my eyes adjusted, I scanned the ground for Loki. I had no idea how long I'd been unconscious. The sun was low in the sky, though, so I'd lost most of the day. I was thirsty, but my canteen was split, my rucksack and my CamelBak torn to shreds.

I stood on shaky legs and moved rocks aside carefully, looking for any sign of Loki. I tried to listen for whimpering or panting, but I heard nothing but a loud ringing. I probably wouldn't have heard him even if he were barking. I wondered if my eardrums had burst.

"Loki," my voice creaked out, triggering a fit of coughing that pushed me back down onto my hands and knees. In the distance, across the valley, I saw tracer fire tickling the sky. Operation Hunting Dog was underway and my dog and I were nowhere near it. I'd screwed up big time. I'd lost control of Loki just when it mattered most.

On hands and knees I moved through the rubble of the cave, sweeping my arms over the rocks, trying to search in some kind of pattern, but I wasn't trained in this. Loki would have crawled through hell to find me, so I kept crawling, through the pain and the ringing and the fear, looking for him.

I thought of our training, how I commanded Loki with hand gestures and with the order "seek, seek." I felt his toy in my pocket, still tucked neatly where it was always tucked. All the search patterns we practiced, and now I was the one doing the searching. I touched the toy through the fabric of my pants. It was comforting, a reminder of what I was trained to do.

"Come on, Gus," I told myself. "Seek. Seek. Get him. Go."

I crept through the rocks. Without my ears, with my eyes stinging, I even tried to sniff at the air, hoping to catch a whiff of dog. I moved slowly, painfully slowly. I didn't want to miss a spot. I imagined how Loki must have felt on all those searches, disappointed every moment that he hadn't found anything, hopeful that the next moment he would.

I was starting to lose hope when I saw movement, a tiny rise and fall of dust. I scurried over to it, and it was Loki, breathing laboriously beneath a slab of rock. I heaved the debris off him and looked down. His eyes were closed. I felt around his head and legs, checking him for injuries. I carefully peeled off his body armor — it was burned and studded with holes where bits of shrapnel from the bomb had hit it. Loki had a wound, right in his belly. It was bleeding.

I hugged Loki close to me, rummaged in my pocket, and found a bandage. I packed the wound with it as best I could to stop the bleeding. I pressed my ear to his chest, but the ringing was still so bad, I couldn't hear anything, certainly not the fading heartbeat of a wounded dog. I had to get him to a medic.

"You're an original gangsta," I quoted Chang. "Come on, dog. Stay with me. Stay with me, Marine."

I lifted him up into a fireman's carry over my shoulders, like I'd done a hundred times in training. Two hundred, maybe. He weighed less than an ammo can filled with concrete. I could do this. I could carry him out of here.

I started picking my way carefully down the slope, back toward the other side of the valley. My leg throbbed with pain. It was over a mile back to the medevac site, and I didn't know how long I could carry my best friend like this. But I had to try. You never leave a marine behind.

CHAPTER 23

FAMILY REUNION

The images came in fragments — marines shouting and the spinning blades of a helicopter, a gleam of sunset off the mountains, the shadow of a tail gunner against the ground below. I heard the whine of mortar fire, or maybe it was the screech of an aircraft's wheels touching down.

I heard my name. I heard Loki's name.

Bright lights shined in my eyes.

I saw the bomber and his terrified face, the wire in his hand, a flash of light, Loki leaping in front of it.

Chang's face appeared and faded. He told a joke I couldn't quite remember. I wanted to laugh.

I slept.

I felt the weight of a ton of rocks crushing my legs. I kicked free of them, and they fell away like paper. My eyes bolted open to the soft morning light. A pile of crumpled sheets lay on the floor next to my hospital bed.

I stared down at my bare feet, pale on the end of my burned legs, poking out of my hospital gown. Stitches ran like a nasty zipper up my thigh. I was alive, in a hospital. I had all my limbs. Something was beeping — a monitor next to my bed. My heart was racing.

A nurse came in, her hair tied back in the Navy bun, tight.

"Calm down, Corporal," she whispered. "You're okay now. You're in Germany."

"Loki!" I screamed. "Help Loki!"

Her face tightened into a mask of worry. My mouth felt like it was full of cotton. My hand was gripping a button, like a detonator. I pressed the button. Relief washed over me, darkness.

"That's okay." The nurse sounded a million miles away. "You just rest."

When I woke, the shades were drawn. Through a sliver of window, I saw only a reflection of the blinking lights in the room. It was night. The button I had pressed lay beside me. It was attached to a tube that led to a bag that led to another tube that was stuck into my arm. It must have been for a painkiller. If I pressed the button I'd get another dose. I let it sit there. I wanted a clear head.

I was in Germany. I didn't know how I got there. I remembered fleeing with Loki. He was hurt. I was hurt. I remembered collapsing into the dirt in Afghanistan during Operation Hunting Dog. I remembered the marines came to get me. Vasquez. He was there. That's all I remembered. But now I was in a military hospital in Germany. Where was Loki?

My legs itched and ached. My head was pounding, like someone was driving nails in just behind my eyes. I looked over at the button, tempted to press it, to go back to sleep.

But I had to find Loki. I had to talk to someone who could tell me what happened to him. I tried to sit up. I got so that my back was resting against the wall behind me and my knees were up. It took all the strength I had.

"Gus!" my little brother Zach burst into the room, clutching some sort of purple candy bar. Was this another crazy dream? "You're awake!" He turned back into the hall-way. "Mom! Gus is awake!"

My mother came scurrying into the room after my brother. She looked about a million years older than when

I'd last seen her, but her face broke into a wide smile and she crossed the room in two steps, locking me in a powerful hug. It hurt like crazy, but she was crying and laughing, and I just gritted my teeth and let her hug me. Zach joined in, and even though it hurt, it also felt great to let my family hug me. I guess feeling two opposite feelings at once wasn't just something that happened in war. It could happen in a bed in a hospital room.

"Looks like you fought some dragons," Zach said.

"I guess I did," I told him. "No treasure, though."

"I'm so glad you're okay," my mother said. "When they called and told us to fly to Germany . . . I thought the worst." She started crying again.

"I'm sorry, Mom. I . . ." A lump formed in my throat. I didn't know what to tell her. I'd volunteered to go on the mission that almost killed me. I'd volunteered to put my mother through hell. What words could make that better?

She just hugged me again. And I hugged her back.

There was a tap on the door to the room. We all glanced over at the doorway. A uniformed marine, a guy about my age, stood there, looking grim. He had an MP's insignia on his sleeve. MP. Elf talk for military police. Was I under arrest for running off on my unit during an operation?

"I'm here about Military Working Dog Loki," the grim-faced MP said.

Then I remembered. The MPs ran the military dog kennels here in Germany. And if he was coming to see me about Loki . . .

My mom squeezed my arm and stood. "I'll be right back." She went into the hall to talk to the MP.

"Loki," I groaned. I turned to my brother. "What happened to him?"

He looked away from me. "I'm not supposed to say."

"But you know?"

He didn't answer. He chewed his lip, like he always did when he was fighting to keep a secret.

My eyes shot over to the door. I saw my mom take a clipboard and sign something.

"Mom!" I shouted. "Where's Loki? Where is he?"

My mom came back in, looking serious.

"He saved my life," I told her. I felt tears streaming down my face. "He jumped in front of me when the bomb went off. I need to know" — Pain sliced through my leg like a knife. I clenched my teeth. I was not about to press the button and fall into a hazy sleep again. I needed answers — "what happened to him."

212

"Loki had serious wounds," my mother said. "They said he was unfit to return to service, so . . ."

My breathing came faster. The pain was terrible. I had to hold on. I had to hear what she was telling me.

"So, I just signed the forms . . ."

I clenched my fists. I knew his injuries were bad when I'd carried him. What if they had to put Loki down? To end his pain? What if my mom had just made that decision without me? What if I never got to say good-bye?

" . . . to adopt him," she finished. "I hope that's okay?"

Her eyebrows raised; her lips formed a curious smile.

"I know I should have asked you first, but —"

"He's alive?" I winced as I sat up straighter in bed. "He's . . . he's . . . You adopted him?" All thoughts of pain vanished. The heart-rate monitor beeped wildly.

"Well, I thought you might —" she started, but that's when a bark in the hallway interrupted her.

"Where are his therapy dog papers?" I heard the nurse objecting. "You can't just let any old dog run around here. This is a hospital!"

"Ma'am, this dog is a sergeant in the United States Marine Corps," the MP replied. "And I'm just following his orders."

With a bandage wrapped around his belly and a clunky cast on his front leg, Loki dragged the MP behind him into the room, stubborn as ever. His tail wagged furiously and his eyes shined.

"You can let him off the leash," I told the MP.

My crazy dog bounded across the room, his cast clunking on the floor, and he leaped, like he wasn't hurt at all. He landed smack-dab on top of me in the bed.

"Ooph!" I grunted. Hot needles of pain shot through my whole body, but Loki's giant tongue licked right up my face, and it was like the pain vanished. His tail wreaked havoc on the tubes and bottles around the bed, but I didn't care. I grabbed Loki around the neck and squeezed him to me.

"You saved my life, pal," I whispered to him as I scratched behind his ears. He panted and licked my face again.

Beside the bed, my mother and Zach watched with tearful smiles on their faces. I wanted to explain to them everything that had happened, about the shepherd boy Zach's age, about Loki running off to find a sleeping bag, about Chang and his Chihuahua, about the colonel and the foul-mouthed sergeant and Lieutenant Schu and the frightened bomber in the cave, and about how this crazy, stubborn, goofball dog was the toughest guy I'd ever met, because tough guys know how to play.

I had so much I wanted to say, so many words ready to burst out of me after all this time . . . but I felt so tired. Loki lay down on the bed next to me, his nose resting against my armpit. I looked at him and felt my eyes drifting shut.

"You want me to take Loki down so you're more comfortable in bed?" my mom asked gently.

"No," I whispered. "He can stay up here with me."

And he was still there when I woke up.

AUTHOR'S NOTE

This is a work of fiction. The people and most of the places are products of my imagination. In fact, all kinds of details were invented, but it is based on research into the way military working dogs are deployed.

Dogs have been fighting in people's wars for about as long as people have. Dogs fought with Alexander the Great and with the Roman soldiers in Caesar's armies, and dogs have served as scouts, guards, messengers, and companions in just about every American war since the Revolution of 1776. Dogs are currently still classified as military equipment, but they are the only military equipment that lives and breathes and loves.

In the war in Afghanistan, military working dogs' training

and roles expanded a lot. German shepherds, Belgian Malinois, and Labrador retrievers deploy with all branches of the United States military. Bomb-sniffing dogs guard bases and convoys of trucks; dogs search for explosives and drugs as well as weapons, and some are trained to track down suspected terrorists. There was even a dog on the Navy SEAL mission to get Osama Bin Laden. His name was Cairo. Afterward, he got to meet the president.

The IED detector dog program has greatly expanded the number of bomb-sniffing dogs able to serve with the United States Marines. When they first arrived in Afghanistan, the Marine Corps had less than one hundred dogs with them. By 2012, that number was over six hundred. The dogs' able noses help protect soldiers and civilians alike from deadly hidden bombs, and it has also been shown that they have a positive effect on the morale of the marines they serve with. Just like Loki and Gus, dog handlers can now adopt their canine partners when the dog's service is done.

If you want to learn more about military working dogs, the best overview I found was in Lisa Rogak's *The Dogs of War: The Courage, Love, and Loyalty of Military Working Dogs*. I also learned a lot from *Sergeant Rex: The Unbreakable*

Bond between a Marine and His Military Working Dog by Mike Dowling, who was one of the first Marine Corps dog handlers to deploy to combat in the Middle East in the twenty-first century. In fact, some of what he and Rex went through is a lot more exciting than the stuff I made up!

In order to research for this novel, I relied heavily on the work of others. Aside from *Sergeant Rex*, Alexandra Horowitz's book *Inside of a Dog: What Dogs See, Smell, and Know* showed me a dog's-eye view of the world, and Sebastian Junger's harrowing book, *War*, gave me great insights into life on a remote military outpost in Afghanistan. I read countless newspaper and magazine articles, blog entries, and even Facebook posts, and I spoke with as many soldiers and marines as I could.

I am especially grateful to my editor, Nick Eliopulos, who dreamed up this project and guided me through it, and to David Levithan, who convinced me to do it in the first place. Alex Muñoz answered my dumb questions, and Rye Barcott gave me an encouraging early read (and his excellent book, *It Happened on the Way to War: A Marine's Path to Peace*, certainly inspired!). Lars Dabney's helpful dispatches from the field filled in some gaps, and a few fellows of the Truman National Security Project stepped up with insight when I needed it. However, any errors of fact or failures of imagination in this work are entirely my own.

Lastly, but most of all, thanks to Tim and to Baxter, my favorite dog in the world, who always pulls me away from writing for the important business of play.

FETCH THIS BOOK!

DOG TAGS

BOOK TWO
STRAYS

Chuck and Ajax are partners, and they're good at their job. Chuck leads Ajax through the jungles of Vietnam, and Ajax sniffs out hidden, deadly traps before they can hurt US soldiers.

But the war in Vietnam is ending, and now Chuck is forced to answer two impossible questions: Is his loyalty to Ajax or to the US Army? And just how far is he willing to go to protect his partner?

Find out the answers in the second book of C. Alexander London's DOG TAGS.